S/A

ALL WE KNOW OF HEAVEN

ALL WE KNOW
OF HEAVEN

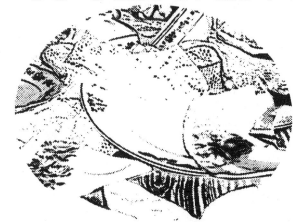

Sue Ellen Bridgers

Banks Channel Books
Wilmington, North Carolina

ISBN 0-9635967-4-8

Library of Congress Catalog Card Number 96-84201

First Edition, 1996

Banks Channel Books
Wilmington, North Carolina

In memory of the women of Renston

who have gone before us

And for Mary Virginia

who is going strong

My life closed twice before its close —
It yet remains to see
If Immortality unveil
A third event to me

So huge, so hopeless to conceive
As these that twice befell.
Parting is all we know of heaven
And all we need of hell.

— Emily Dickinson

ALL WE KNOW OF HEAVEN

CHAPTER ONE

🦋 BETHANY

I was tending the fires in the yard when I first saw him. It was dawn following a cold, clear night, the kind of morning you'd want for a hogkilling. The moon was still out but by then the last stars were slipping backwards in the sky and light was creeping in, tugging at the hidden corners of the shed and dancing on the windows of my aunt Charlotte's kitchen.

I knew who he was because he was with his daddy. Mr. J.C. helped Uncle Mac with hogkilling most every year. He was the best butcher in the county and glad to take a ham in payment, times being so bad.

I kept feeding the fires to keep the water at a boil and pretending not to notice how he was looking at me. I know what he saw. My cheeks and lips already felt chapped and I was wearing a ragged cap and one of Charlotte's old coats. I'd barely pulled a comb through my hair that morning so it was bunched up in tangled curls around my collar.

My best friend Olivia came about then and in a minute Uncle Mac pulled up with more relatives in his truck. They had the slaughter in the back. Charlotte wouldn't let him do the sticking at the house where we could hear. That was Charlotte for you —always protecting us from everything but herself.

"Why, that's Joel Calder," Olivia said to me. "Lord, he's turned out to be good-looking!"

We watched him help my cousins Trax and Davey drag a hog off the truck. They staggered some, carrying it by its feet. He was holding the front end, the gaping throat at his chest. The pig disappeared in the water, bubbling and splashing like the heat had revived it.

"Be quick, boys!" Uncle Mac yelled. "We want to leave the cooking to the ladies." The men chuckled at the mention of women. I knew Olivia and I didn't count. It was the women in the house they were thinking about.

We went inside where Charlotte and Milly Holmes were getting ready to make sausage. From the long row of windows across the back of Charlotte's kitchen, we watched the boys put the pig on a tow sheet and start scraping. They lifted the wet hairs on their knives, then wiped the thick clumps on the grass.

Mr. J.C. went over and slit the hind legs so they could push a long peg behind the tendons to hang the pig by. Then they heaved it on a flatbed and dragged it to the gallows near the wash shed and strung it up. That's when Charlotte sent me out with a pan. I stood back a little while Mac cut the pig down the belly and pulled the slit open to expose the entrails. He cut the heart and lungs out, then slung the liver and bladder across the gallows. I held up the pan to catch the sweetbreads, trying to keep my face turned away from the splattering blood.

He was looking at me then.

I went back in the kitchen to tell Charlotte that Mac said we could come rid the chitlins anytime. I was standing at the window watching Joel's hand go deep into the pig's belly to pull the intestines out when I said it. In a minute, the ropes spilled into the tub at his feet. His hands were slimy with blood.

🌿 JOEL

When she answered Mac, I didn't have time to hear. I was up to my elbows in hog so as soon as I could, I went to the shed to wash but it was thick and stubborn to come off. By that time she was gone and I couldn't remember the sound of her voice.

Trax and me toted the carcass to the table. It was cold as a well digger's ass out there but by then I was sweating under my coat. I kept it on anyhow while I made a cut against the shoulder like Daddy'd showed me.

That Olivia Washburn was with her so I figured they were about the same age. Fifteen maybe, with bodies like women under their coats. She was looking at me. If I'd looked up I could of made our eyes meet. I could of held her there if I'd wanted to but that shoulder meat was thick and I was having a time with it. When I straightened up and pulled the blade free, she was watching me. I knew without looking.

I'd just been home one day. Slept around the clock seeing as I could hardly get a wink on the train. My big brother Ed met me at the depot. It was about midnight but instead of going home, we stopped by the filling station at Hamm's Crossroads and played poker till first light. Let me tell you, I cleaned 'em out! Six and a half bucks! They didn't know I put my allowance on the table every week at Pine Mountain Military Academy.

So I had six dollars and fifty cents free money to buy her something with. A Christmas present. Maybe something for Mama, too. A little bottle of toilet water, nice like she wouldn't get for herself. The rest I'd spend on Bethany. Right then and there I planned it out. I could see it in my mind, like it was a picture show and I was in it.

On Christmas Day, I'd come back, right up to the front door and ring the bell. Charlotte Woodard might be surprised as the dickens but she'd be bound to let me in. I'd stand there in the parlor while she'd go fetch Bethany who'd come quick, like she was waiting somewhere close and secret. She'd be wearing a white dress, one that touched her body everywhere, and she'd look sort of shy, like she wanted to smile but was holding on to it. What would I get her? Gloves because her hands looked raw. A red scarf. Maybe a comb. A fancy one. Someday I would comb that hair. Someday I would touch her everywhere.

It was warming up fast out there between the fires. I opened my jacket and breathed deep. The air smelled like scalding meat and wood smoke. She was gone from the yard so I looked at the closed-up house. The back door was shut tight. She was in there. I knew where to find her.

🌺 CHARLOTTE

To tell the truth I was surprised to see him. Like folks say, out of sight, out of mind. I remembered his reputation though, his being a loner and all. I knew he'd been off at school for awhile— several years, in fact. But now he was home for Christmas.

"He goes to one of those military academies," my friend Milly Holmes told the girls. "I reckon they thought it would do him good." She was stirring a pot of hashlet we were fixing for dinner while Bethany and Olivia rinsed the intestines in the sink.

"Why was that?" Bethany wanted to know.

"Oh, you know how young fellas can be." I was thinking that the less said about that boy, the better.

She was watching him bend over one of the tubs where the men were layering the first hams in salt. When he straightened up, his shoulders strained against his bloody jacket. He looked like his mother's people, big-boned but trim with thick auburn hair and a solemn, careful face.

"He asked me who you were," Olivia said to Bethany. "Just came up and asked like he couldn't be bothered with how-you-do. I told him you were Charlotte and Mac's niece and that you live here with them."

"Well, we have some good help today," I said.

"All the Calders are good at carving," Milly said. "Why, J.C. can whittle anything he's got a mind to — he can get the likeness of a face."

Bethany and Olivia were still watching Joel.

"You girls, get those casings drained," I said to bring them back to business. "Olivia, I want you to take a mess of chitlins home with you."

"Mama'll be obliged," Olivia said.

Milly clunked her spoon against the stew pot. "Just last week, I saw a picture in the paper of all these folks lined up outside a soup kitchen in New York City, and here we are with hashlet and chitlins. It makes me glad to be from farming folks."

"Well, maybe Mr. Roosevelt will put an end to those lines before things get any worse," I said. "Now let me fry some cornbread and we'll be ready to eat. We've got some hungry men of our own to feed."

BETHANY

They filed into the dining room in their stocking feet, their wool socks bulging around their toes. Their faces looked raw with cold and their hands were red and dripping from the pan of hot water we'd put on the back porch for them to wash in. They'd left their jackets piled over their boots so they were coatless in the dining room, their old flannel shirts and long-johns exposed. Sitting on Charlotte's velvet cushioned chairs, their elbows clear of her white tablecloth, they looked out of place and uncomfortable, even Mac who'd paid for everything in sight.

Olivia and I brought in the dishes: the steaming bowls of hashlet, stewed tomatoes, mashed potatoes, collards with fatback curling in the pot liquor.

"Come on and sit with us," Trax said like he didn't know women don't sit at the table on hogkilling day. Or else he wanted to embarrass Olivia and me for being there at all.

"This is just for the men," I said, my cheeks hot.

"We've got to get the cornbread," Olivia told him.

"Well, come back and eat," Mac said. "Tell Milly and Charlotte, too. There's room."

The men laughed and started the food around the table. Milly and Charlotte came in bringing coffee, a pound cake and a bowl of canned peaches. They smoothed their hair with their hands, flung their aprons aside, brought plates and silverware from the sideboard and pulled up chairs to the ends of the table, Charlotte beside Mac, Milly beside Uncle George. Olivia sat next to Davey and I found myself pulled in between the two older boys.

"Aren't you going to eat?" Trax asked, holding the bowl of hashlet above my empty plate. The food had stopped with me. I took the bowl carefully, in both hands, then realized I couldn't spoon it out that way.

"Here," Joel Calder said. I saw his hand on the spoon, watched the stew scooped onto my plate, felt the pressure of his fingers against mine as he took the bowl from me.

"Thank you," I said but I didn't turn to him.

"I'm Joel," he said, leaning toward me a little. His skin was pale and fresh with the smell of blood and water. "And you're Bethany." His mouth was close to my ear.

Even my name felt new.

CHAPTER TWO

 MENA

When that chile was just a little thing, I's the one went with them once a week to do the cleanin and the wash. They went over there other times for certain but that don't bother me none. I had my plate full anyhow.

You could smell it in the house, I mean the sickness her poor mama had and her the light-hearted one, the prettiest, too, and sweet. I will say Miss Hatsy was good, leastways accordin to what I know. Won't time for her to do but so much bad, I don't reckon, crossin over young like she done. All she ever did to worry a soul was marry up with that sorry Warren Newell which won't so much bad as wrong-headed. More marries than do's well, that's the truth. I don't know as nobody tried to stop her. Didn't nobody want to say no to her, her bein so good natured and all.

In due time they gets a baby, this little girl named out of the Bible and all at once, it seem like, Miss Hatsy she sick with the nightsweats and achin in her chest and she get thin and the doctor say she done et up inside. I seen her nipple oozin and her arms swoll plump and soft. Look like if you stuck a pin in her, she'd bust.

After that, me and Miz Bess and Miss Charlotte be the ones seein to things. We brung dinner in Miss Charlotte's automobile, the first one I ever rode in best I can recall. Cold roast chicken, tomatoes to slice, ham biscuits, custards in little glass cups that jiggled and clicked in the basket while we rode. Before long, them custards was the only thing Miss Hatsy had a hankerin for. Little ole egg custards with a sprinkle of nutmeg on the top. She couldn't hardly swallow nothin else.

They started in the house while I done the wash under the shed in the backyard. The chile was there. Five, maybe six years old, I reckon she was, and she come runnin to help me. I didn't never mind. She was good to talk to while I done the wash. Sometimes Miss Hatsy set in the back porch shade and watched while her private things passed through my hands to her girl's. She'd see them up there on the line, flappin like little wings. Sometimes she'd call out. Be like a little whisper rustlin in them blue hydrangeas bushes beside the porch but Bethany would hear and go runnin. I seen her stop just fore pouncin. You know how chil'ren do, runnin straight on and bangin the livin daylights outa you. But she'd stop. She knowed to stop.

Seein that, I got to where I hugged that chile myself. Manys the time I bent down, plumb worn out from the washin, and scooped her up like she be one of mine. She was a tiny thing back then, won't hardly big as a minute.

You can love on a white chile till she be seven or eight, I reckon, and then it's keep away and call her Miss. Little ladies, they pretends like, 'cept for her. Not her. I can still call her precious and honey lamb. Whatever I wants, I can say to her and I do.

🌿 BETHANY

I knew Mama was going to die. I heard Charlotte say so but I didn't truly know what dying meant. I didn't understand how slow it could be, all those long days of quiet with Mama lying still, the shades sucking around a little breeze, her face covered with a cool cloth I wrung out and brought to her. She didn't take me up anymore and I heard a soft whistle of breath when I got too close, like she was afraid of me, of what I could do to her, maybe what I had already done.

It was Mena who hugged. Her arms felt alive, her heart-beat pounded in my ear. I asked her everything because I could trust this woman who had a root against every evil, who knew the time without looking at the clock, who felt the spirit move every Sunday and jumped up shaking and dancing and singing till finally she'd come to herself in the aisle with her new hat turned backwards on her head and her dress wringing wet.

"Everybody gonna cross over sometime, chile, but not right here this minute," she said when I asked her if I was going to die, too. She was lifting white cloth out of the steaming water. She dipped it again, sloshing her heavy breasts and dark muscled arms. "Don't you go botherin yourself none."

Her arms glistened under the soapsuds. "I tell you the truth, you's lookin more and more like this here side of the family every day. A pretty girl. Now you be glad of that."

I watched the sheets snake out of the wringer, permanently wrinkled but squeezed dry enough for us to drag the willow basket to the line.

Mena talked on: "Take my Peaches. She come out of me white as this here sheet. It's the truth. That old granny woman say, 'Whoa' and leave me there, don't tie off or nothin. I got to do it myself or else call Watteau. Now he come runnin from the yard — don't no man stay in the house if he can help it — and he see Aunt Lyda packin up and her bleached out and quivery round the mouth. If he han't heard me hollerin, he'd a thought I's dead. The baby, too."

Mena lifted a sheet with a groan, flipped it over the line to keep it out of the dirt and began pinning it straight.

"So Watteau come. He look. He puts a knife through the cord and tie it off best he can. Puts the baby on my belly and her just bawlin. Then he goes after your Mama Bess. She the one washes up Peaches. About then, the after start comin and, law, I think I's havin another one. But Miz Bess, she push down on my belly and hold the bucket and here it come, here it come. Watteau buried it in the woods, deep so no animal goin get it. Hold on to this here sheet."

"He buried the baby?" I cried.

"Lawsy no, chile. He bury the after. The baby fine. You knows Peaches."

"She's not white anymore."

"That the truth. She darkened up real nice, but she still don't look like none of us. Not like you resembles them Malones. Why, you's your mama all over agin."

When I went to Charlotte's to live, Mena was there. Mama had been dead more than a year then and I'd been alone with Daddy all that time until Charlotte took me away from him. Charlotte made me wear underpants. She cut the mats out of my hair and gave me a white iron bed with a pink spread in the little front room above the porch. Mena hugged me hard.

🌸 CHARLOTTE

The room was stifling. Not a breath of air anywhere so I tugged at a window first thing. The paint had been broken at the sill so I managed to nudge the dusty pane up six inches before it stuck. The heat felt heavy on my hands and I stood there a minute looking out at the dusty, unswept yard, and wondering what to do.

When I turned around, Bethany was standing on the other

side of the bed. We both looked at her daddy.

"How long has he been like this?" I asked her.

"Since Saddy."

She'd just turned seven, a skinny dingy little thing. I remember thinking her arms and legs looked like cornstalks.

"It's three syllables. Sa-tur-day." I poked at him. "Warren? Warren, I'm taking Bethany home with me and this time, it's for good. You're not fit to bring up a child. Do you hear me?" His shoulder felt like a sponge.

"He don't."

"Doesn't!" I could see he wasn't going to fight me this time. There was nothing else to do but take her. "Hurry up now and get your belongings," I said.

She didn't budge. "I tried to clean him up," she said.

"I know you did, honey." I said. But there he was, one arm flung behind him, palm up like he'd just been released from a restraint. His curled hand looked so innocent, like a baby's palm you'd want to lay your finger into.

"I'll get somebody over here to tend to him. Now you get your belongings and come on home with me. Davey and Patsy need somebody to hold on to besides their mama."

She didn't move.

"I can't stand here all day," I said finally. "I've got things at home." I went around the bed and got her hand. "I'll help you pack. Is there a suitcase somewhere? What about a box and some newspaper?"

While she collected her things, I packed Sister's china. To tell the truth, I was surprised he hadn't smashed it up or pawned it. He'd always been worthless but now that he was drinking bad, there was no telling what he'd do.

That's why I took her — because he couldn't stop me like he did Mama. She'd tried to get Bethany several times after Sister died, said everything she knew to say, but he wouldn't. He thought he couldn't live without her. "The only thing of Hatsy's I've got left," he said, like the child was a plate on the shelf or a piece of land he could leave fallow.

She was watching me wrap the last saucer.

"This is yours," I told her. "You mama would want it to go to you — I'm certain of that. You can use it yourself when you get married and have a home of your own."

"I never would," Bethany said, but there was the beginning of a smile crinkling her mouth.

"That's one thing you'll change your mind about. Now let's go. Your Uncle Mac's going to be wondering what's become of us." I wanted to get home to my own children.

🌹 BETHANY

He'd been drunk three days when Charlotte came. I didn't cry. I wanted to but not in front of Charlotte who always hated Daddy. Standing there looking at him and listening to her tell me how it was going to be, I clenched my hands in my pockets so hard I couldn't feel them. When I let go, there was a prickly feeling in my fingers, so hot I wanted to lick them cool. Mostly I wanted Daddy to move. I wanted him to wake up and say something Charlotte would have to listen to, something to make her stop.

But at least, he wasn't thrashing around, yelling and carrying on like he'd been doing the night before. When I tried to tie him up in a sheet to keep him from hurting himself, he caught me so hard in my stomach I had to let go. The bruised place hurt every time I moved fast. He didn't mean to do it. I knew that. He didn't mean to pee in the bed, either, but he couldn't help himself.

I could see Charlotte was serious about taking me with her. She made me put my clothes in Daddy's old leather satchel. Even half empty, it was heavy. She packed Mama's dishes in a box. I thought she was taking them for herself but she said they were for me, for when I got married.

She was in a hurry but I still wanted to wake up my daddy.

I went back to his room and looked at him. He had on his good shirt and his suit pants he wouldn't let me get off him. He smelled like pee and puke and his hair was sweaty. Spit had puddled on the pillow where his mouth hung open. I could see there wasn't any use.

"Bye, Daddy. I'll be back directly," I whispered to him. I meant it, too.

The rumbling engine of Charlotte's car jumped into the quiet. At the back door I stopped, thinking I saw movement in the house, Mama's shadow floating between the rooms, but I knew it was the shimmer of dust rising in the heat outside.

Charlotte honked her car horn, calling me away. I went. I wanted a hot biscuit enough to go anywhere. I wanted to hold Charlotte's little baby. I wanted something in my arms as bad as anything. My hand on the doorknob shook.

"Good-bye, house," I said, then closed the door behind me. That is how I went.

🌸 CHARLOTTE

I wanted to buy her dresses. That's where my mind was — on buying things. Well, how could I let people see she'd come from squalor?

"After awhile, we'll go downtown," I said. I had my back to her while she ate pancakes at the table. She was licking syrup off her fingers and taking long, gurgling swallows of milk.

"We'll go shopping," I went on, although I really wanted to comment on her manners. She ate noisily, like a little pig snuffling and snorting. "We'll get you a pretty Sunday dress and some new shoes. Then we'll look for material for school dresses. I can make those."

"I'm not going to school," she said.

I just stared at her. She'd fallen asleep on the way home the day before and slept right through till morning. A tangle of hair was matted on her cheek, caught in road dust and syrup. I could see I'd probably have to cut it out.

I went to get her plate. "Of course not now. It's summertime. But come September, you'll be going."

"I hate school. Daddy said I didn't have to go, ever again."

"That's a fool talking," I said. "Everybody who's given the opportunity goes to school."

"Not if they don't want to. Daddy says I'm smart enough. Too smart for him, he says."

"I don't doubt that." I was trying to stay calm. "But you're here with us now and you're going to school in the fall, so you might as well go in something decent." I slid the sticky plate under the water and left it there.

"You're a witch, Charlotte. That's what you are. Daddy said so. He says all you Malones are mean. All except my mama."

I turned to her then. "I want you to go upstairs and take a bath. Then I want you to put on the nicest dress you have because we'll be going downtown in a little bit."

"I want to go home."

"This is your home now."

"It's not! I want Daddy!"

"Well, he obviously doesn't want you, Bethany. He doesn't take care of you and you're not supposed to be taking care of him."

"He gets sick sometimes, that's all."

"He gets drunk."

We eyed each other across the table. There's no saying who's the most stubborn, then or now.

"And about school," I said, "if you don't go, the authorities will come and take you to an orphanage. That's where children have to stay when they misbehave so bad nobody in their family wants them. Now you take yourself upstairs and into that bathtub."

She left the table without another word but I can remember how her eyes looked, how for a moment they betrayed her. She believed me. I washed her plate and put a ham shank on to boil for supper. I was trembling all the time. It occurred to me to take her out to Mama and Papa at Rowe's Crossing or to George and Lucille where she'd have cousins her age. But Mama wasn't able and Lucille, as good as she is, wasn't born a Malone. It's the women who do the raising and I wanted her raised by one of us.

After a minute, I heard the water running upstairs, heard the pipes shuddering hard when it stopped, then a cringing sound from high in the throat like an animal's whimper when there's no deep breath left to draw.

I went up and peeped in at the bathroom door and there she was, her frail shoulders huddled forward in the tub, her unwashed face streaked with tears.

I went in, knelt beside the tub and found the washcloth in the water. I rubbed soap on it and touched her neck. She shivered but then turned her face toward me, her eyes closed and head still just like she'd learned years ago when it was her mother's hand that bathed her cheek. The cloth separated us but I felt the bone, the flutter of pulse beneath her jaw, the hard ridge of her shoulder. Neither of us said a word.

She was still until I pulled her up and wrapped a towel around her. Then her arms went up, her legs lifted around my thighs and I was holding her. Her damp face was against my neck, her wet body clinging, her hard knees pressed to my sides. She smelled of soap, of cool dampness and the sun-dried towel.

What am I going to do with her? I wondered, feeling her grip tighten. She's not a baby I can make into anything I want to. This branch is already bent.

I sighed and lowered my head to rest against her wet hair. She would always be Warren Newell's daughter. What came from him was living in her somewhere, but she was Harriet's, too — and mine.

I could feel our breathing, how it slowly fell into the same rhythm, the same pulse. Only Bethany's heart raced faster, a child's heart. I held her a long time.

All We Know of Heaven

CHAPTER THREE

 ED

I know Joel intended to buy her something, the same way
he said he'd get a little do-dad for Mama but come time, he didn't.
The weekend before Christmas he went out to Billy Hamm's to
play poker and lost a bundle. Maybe I should of made it right — it
was five dollars he lost — but by God, he had to grow up sometime. Always acting like he knew everything. Well, there we were,
all struggling to hang on to a dime any way we could, banks closing left and right, people losing all they had, and he ought to
known Billy Hamm won't gonna let him walk away a second time.
Folks like the Hamm's that still got money keep a tight hold on it
and goddammit, that's how.

Come Christmas, I let him put his name on my present for
Mama — a length of cloth my girlfriend Annette picked out so
Mama could make herself a new dress. I got Daddy a pipe and Joel
signed on with that, too. Well, hell, I didn't want to see his face
Christmas morning otherwise.

Not that we saw much of him as it was. He wasn't one to
stay in the house, not even in the wintertime. He'd roam around
in the woods, muck the barn. Shoot pool when he could get to

Lawrence. Sometimes he'd take the truck and be gone hours at a time. Daddy didn't say a word against it that I ever heard. There again, sometimes I'd find him out in the cold on the front steps staring out at nothing. We let him be.

Course, come summertime he was the one you could count on to spend nights under the shelter and keep watch over the cur-ing fires. Did that when he was just a little fella. Hell, the next morning he'd be out there behind a mule or bent low priming. He wasn't afraid of a day's work, I can tell you that.

Another thing, he'd take the highest rafters when we were barning or taking out. He'd hang up there where the air's so hot and close you can't get a deep breath and your legs burn from holding steady. Then, like I say, he'd want to go to town and stay all hours. I don't know when he got any sleep. Course, that was before Bethany.

The last night he was home that Christmas he told me about her. We were sparring in the barn. We'd shed our shirts and dropped our suspenders and we were dancing around in the cold. Just lantern light to see by. Joel couldn't sneak gloves into his duf-fle bag at school, just wrap, so we weren't punching hard.

"A left jab and a straight right?" I tried to do it but he went after me in a clench. He had my arms tight.

"You smell like a goddamn barn," I said to him.

"After tomorrow, it's a cold shower every fucking morn-ing."

"Well, you can heat a pan of water here."

He let me go. "Ed, I met this girl."

I wiped my face and neck with the end of a tow sack. "At school? How'd you do that?"

"Naw, here. Charlotte and Mac Woodard's niece. Bethany something."

Hell, here he'd taken a shine to a sweet young thing and didn't hardly know her name. I went to bouncing on the scattered hay. "I know who you mean. She plays basketball," I told him. "Long legs, nice bosom. Good ball handler, too."

He jabbed at me then. Hard near-misses at my head and

shoulders. "Goddammit, don't talk about her like that," he said.

I grabbed his arms and held him while he kept on thrashing around. "It's okay, little brother," I said to him. He was straining hard. "I didn't mean nothing." I could feel the blood pounding in his neck. I knew how worked up he could get over the least little thing.

He calmed down some but I still held him tight. I knew better than to let go too soon. "It's just a little practice match," I said. "You're showing me all you've learned. You're good. I bet you're the best at that school of yours. When you come home this summer, maybe you can do some boxing over in Lawrence. Lately they've been putting up a ring in a warehouse and getting some yahoos to fight a big bag of guts they haul in from somewhere. No brains but he's a strong son of a bitch. Mean, too. Most of them boys get their heads bashed in right quick cause they don't know shit about boxing. But you now, you got technique, you got knowhow. You could stay in there."

I eased my arm loose from his chest and waited a little. Then I let him go altogether. I said, "That Bethany Newell is a fine looking girl, Joey. You ought to be glad other people think so."

"I'm going to get her," he said. He pulled at the knot on his wrappings till the bandage started rolling off his hand. He looked worn out. "I'm going to."

"I can see that," I told him.

🌹 BETHANY

I felt him everywhere. It was like a little fever or an itch on my skin. All through the Christmas holidays, I'd glance him out of the corner of my eye, then turn and look boldly at another person, somebody hardly handsome at all who happened to have hair the color of rust or a laugh that made me start.

No boy had touched me then, except once a long time ago

when Douglas Watson surprised us both by plopping a damp punch-smelling kiss right on my mouth at the end of the fifth grade Valentine's Day party Charlotte gave to make sure I was being friendly with the children she approved of. I believe Douglas was more impressed with the party — the candles and valentines decorated with paper doilies on little tables, a three course dinner before we danced to records on the Victrola, the corsage his mother had bought me — than he was excited by me because after that he didn't try to touch me at all.

So now I didn't know what to do, caught like I was for the first time in a strange, dreamy place that seemed to mean everything or nothing. I didn't know which. It was like I couldn't wake up and yet I was alert to everything. My skin tingled. Charlotte had the house all decorated, too, so that made everything look different. Possible.

One night I dreamed I was dancing and woke up to find my cold bare arms stretched out to a partner who disappeared just as my eyes opened. I stayed in the dream all the next day, living the dance, feeling myself in his arms, hearing music in my head.

None of that brought him to me. Well, I wasn't surprised. After all, I hadn't encouraged him in the least, holding back like I did the day of the hogkilling. The next time I saw him, I would look him straight in the eyes — they were gray eyes and deep-set but I couldn't bring back their exact expression, couldn't remember the true feel of them. Next time, I'd look. And talk my head off.

Oh, I wanted to tell somebody. I ached to say his name but I couldn't. Not to Mac who would tease, or to Charlotte who would want to know everything I was thinking and feeling. Not even to Olivia who just wanted to get away. She wanted us to go to Raleigh, maybe even Richmond, and get jobs after high school. She'd been planning it for years and she would see Joel Calder as an obstacle. There was nobody and so I kept to myself, longing so raw in me there was no soothing it.

J.C.

I went to my boy's graduation. His mama wouldn't budge from home and Ed had the spring planting to get finished so I went by myself.

The graduation was out there on the marching field with them fieldstone buildings all around it. Being as it was a military school, it looked something like a prison except for the trees. There's some fine oaks there. Some locusts, too. Old trees.

It was a hot day. After a considerable amount of speeches, the boys walked up to get their diplomas. Then the bugler played, they threw their hats up in the air, and it was over with. Joel and me walked over to his room which looked like it did four years back when I brought him there the first time. Like a cell, as empty as that. He had everything he owned in his duffle bag so I knew that room hadn't never looked much different, nothing like a home. It was so bare and plain, it hurt me to see it.

Boys were rambling in the halls, saying their good-byes. Joel did the same so I sat down on his cot to give a little pain I'd been having time to pass. Mostly it ran down my arm to my fingers. This quick flood of nausea came behind it but that passed. After a spell, I got to where I could grip a fist again. A minute or two, was all. While I waited, I thought about Joel sleeping there on that cot, curled up like a baby because more than likely he was too long for it. I can tell you it was a sorry sight.

I used to check on the children at night, starting back when Ed was a little fella and suffering so bad with the croup. Many's the night Emma and me were up stoking the woodstove to get enough steam for that child to breathe. He'd choke and hack like he was about to rattle himself to death. So I started checking on him even when he was quiet and four years later when Joel came along, him too. Before the lamp gave out, I'd go in and cover shoulders and feet. I loved the sight of them in that unsteady light. I liked to touch their hair and hands. I loved their skinny sleeping backs.

Then we had Alice who barely got to outgrow the cradle. I can hardly recall her anymore, leastways how she looked sleeping. She was gone so quick and then Emma was sick, suffering with the bleeding that ended up meaning a train trip to Richmond and one of them female operations. After that she was so full of frights and longings, I never knew from one minute to the next how I'd find her — crying or smiling. I don't reckon she knew herself.

I wrote to the doctor in Richmond, explaining how she was and he wrote back after a long while, telling me how the operation had been a success. Hadn't the incision healed? Hadn't her bleeding stopped? He didn't speak to the fact that, still young and able, she acted like an invalid most of the time. Turned away from me when I needed her most, and about as often, fell in my arms full of tears. I couldn't seem to comfort her with hands or soothing words. I'm not blaming her though. Or Joel either. There's pain so deep there's no reaching it.

I kept on resting there on his bunk after the ache had eased off, waiting for him to come back. I wondered if he was as worried about leaving as I was to take him home, it being permanent and all. The school had calmed him down some, best I could tell. He'd kept by the rules and behaved himself right off the bat but my mind couldn't help fretting about what he was going to do now that he was leaving for good with some boxing medals and a high school diploma. Times being so hard, I knew it won't worth the paper it was written on, not to get a job with.

Well, he could farm with Ed and me if he couldn't do better. Maybe he'd go to Baltimore where we've got relations. If I'd had the money, I reckon I'd of considered sending him on to college but that wouldn't be fair to Ed who wanted more schooling himself. Besides, we couldn't just keep on sending him off.

I could tell my color was coming back. I squeezed my fingers, released. All right. I heard Joel in the hall so I stood up, ready to go. I was taking my boy home.

CHAPTER FOUR

 MILLY

Charlotte invited her family for supper the night of the Red Banks Chautauqua and of course, she included Wilton and me and our little ones. I told her we'd be there with bells on. Her family all accepted, too: Lucille and George and theirs and Bess and Rowe from out in the country.

"I just wish Rose and hers were here," Charlotte said when we were all crowded into her dining room. She was always wishing her sister didn't live so far away.

"I don't know where in the world you'd put them," Lucille said.

"We'd find a place." It was just like Charlotte to be aggravated and happy all at the same time.

I knew she and Mena had spent all afternoon in the kitchen boiling vegetables and frying chicken. Then she'd taken a cool bath and put on her new gray dotted swiss which was already wet down the back.

"Mena, bring in the biscuits," she called when everybody was seated.

"There's a magician tonight, Papa Rowe," Traxler said. "I

bet he's going to saw somebody in two!"

"Just don't you go up there," Rowe said. "I saw that trick fail once. There was screaming and blood flowing —"

"Rowe Malone, hush up," Bess said. "That's nothing to talk about at the table. Besides, it's a boldface lie he's telling or I'd of heard it before."

"There's a song and dance team, too," Patsy said. "I saw them practicing this afternoon."

"You didn't get in the way down there, did you?" Charlotte said.

"Now that's what I'm interested in," George said, rolling his eyes at the boys. "None of that speechifying for me. I want a pretty dancing girl."

"George, you're as bad as Papa," Charlotte said, smiling big. She was so happy to have them all together like that.

At quarter of eight we walked over to the auditorium. The young people strode along in front, in a hurry to get there but held back because of Bess. She was leaning hard on her Sunday cane and taking shallow breaths we all pretended not to hear.

BETHANY

When my cousin Lizzie and I met Olivia in front of the auditorium it was already half-full and sweltering.

"I thought you'd never get here," Olivia said, navigating us through the crowded doorway.

"Let's don't sit at the front," Lizzie said. "I couldn't stand it if I was called on. I wouldn't go up there for a million dollars!"

We settled in seats a few rows from the stage while the auditorium quickly filled around us. Folding seats squeaked at their hinges and cardboard fans advertising the funeral home in Lawrence made little gulping sounds as they moved. The lights flickered once. A baby wailed and then was quiet.

"Look," Olivia whispered, "there're those Calder boys."

She was motioning across the aisle toward the side section.

The lights flickered again and I blinked with them, focusing on the close-clipped hair around Joel's ear, his strong, tanned neck against the edge of his shirt collar. He was as handsome as I remembered and I studied his profile, hoping my stare would make him notice me. I watched him lean over to say something to his brother and that's when my eye moved past him for a second and I saw a sloping shoulder, a thin corded neck with tufts of graying hair sprouting from it and a square jaw jutting from a frayed collarless shirt. I stared, my hands still in my lap, my face flushed hot.

The auditorium lights went down again and the room was dark except for pale rectangles of twilight through the open windows. The row of footlights on the stage came on and the curtain began its slow swishing disappearance into the wings. I could still see the sagging outline of the man's cheek, his eye.

On stage, the magician swung his cape and released a pair of white doves. The light glinted on their wings as they ascended. The audience around me gasped and applauded above the tinny music. He swirled his cape again and the doves were back in their cage. There were two cages, two sets of doves.

"How did he do that?" Lizzie whispered but I didn't answer.

Instead, I held on to the narrow wooden armrests between the seats, determined not to bolt. My toes drew up in my Sunday shoes, wanting to move. The bones in my fingers ached, holding still. Across the aisle Joel had slouched in his seat. He was watching the show, oblivious of me. Then he was laughing, leaning forward to get a better view, whispering to his brother. I watched him, forced myself to see only his profile, the curl of his lip, the sparkle of light on his eye, his hand brushing through the hair on his forehead.

I would not look at my daddy.

MAC

The show was over by nine-thirty and we walked back home in the dark. It was a hot evening, one of those nights that barely cools off before dawn. Charlotte wanted everybody to come in and have a slice of banana cake but George thought it was too late. We were standing there on the porch, some ready to go, others deciding to let them when a voice came to us out of the dark.

"Evening," the man said. "How you all getting on?"

"Evening," I said. Not knowing who it was, I thought he'd move along.

"I been planning to come by," the voice said. It was the durndest thing, familiar but with no name attached to it.

"Who is that?" Lucille asked. She leaned over the rail to get a better look.

"I know who it is," Charlotte said. She was standing closest to the steps. "Warren, you've got no business here," she said as cold as ice.

"Where's my child?" the voice called out suddenly. "Where's my baby?" He sounded like he was about to cry.

"You can't come moaning around here and expect us to kowtow," Charlotte said.

He staggered on up the walk toward us. He looked sick and helpless but that didn't mean we could trust him.

"Stay right there," I said.

"Well, let him talk," Lucille said. "I, for one, want to hear what he's got to say."

"I think we ought to sit down," Bess said. "Charlotte, let the man take a seat."

"I will not, Mama," Charlotte said. "This is my house and he is not welcome in it, not till hell freezes over which it never will."

"I got something to say to my little girl," Warren cried. I could see his face then, trembly and pale as a ghost. His eyes looked like empty sockets. He kept on coming, one slumped shoulder turned to us.

"You say it from right there," I said. "I don't want to have to get the police."

"I want to talk to him alone." Bethany came out of the deepest corner of the porch. I think Lizzie had been holding her still all that time.

"No, I won't have it," Charlotte said. "You mind me, Bethany. This one time you mind me."

"He's my daddy," Bethany said. She could be as determined as Charlotte — that's one thing she'd learned.

"He's a drunk," Charlotte said. "Mac and me, we're your family now."

"I want to talk to him," Bethany said. She and Charlotte were standing side by side on the edge of the porch, looking out at him. Bethany was already a fraction taller, but she was thinner and as frisky as a colt. She seemed to be pulling away from all that held her.

"We'll walk," she said. "I'll be back in a little while."

Everybody heard Charlotte draw in her breath, shuddering with it, but she stayed still. We all did. We watched as they passed under the streetlight on the corner, then melted into the thick shadows of the summer night. In less than a minute, they were gone.

🌺 WARREN

You tell me what I had to lose. First God took my Hatsy and then the Malones took my baby girl. There won't much left after that.

Looked like all of them was there on the porch. Bess and Rowe still living. Charlotte looking healthy as a horse. I reckon she was too mean to die.

I figured to wait till everybody went home so I'd have just

Charlotte and Mac to deal with. And Bethany, of course. That's what I'd come for — to see exactly how she'd growed up and to tell her my news. But I was shaking so bad by the time I got there, I thought I'd best get on with it.

I knew which one was her. I watched them walking home so I was certain. Between the two girls, it was easy because one had that blunt face belonging to Lucille Benson's people and the other one — God, she was Hatsy all over again. In her walk, the way she throwed her head back to laugh, the sound itself full of crying and singing all at once. Hatsy always cried when she laughed. Hearing my child, I wanted to reach out of the dark and catch that sound. I wanted to pull it into my own chest where no laughing had been for a long time.

"Evening," I said and it was too late to pass on by.

Charlotte knew it was me. I reckon she'd been looking behind herself for the devil all these years. She'd been expecting me.

Bethany came off the porch looking like an angel in a flowered dress and a fine ribbon in her hair. She took my hand and before I knew it, we were walking away from them. By Jove, we were!

🌺 BETHANY

"I wrote you letters," he said. "Two of them, and you never answered. I poured my heart out."

"I never got them," I said. I felt like I'd been holding my breath for hours, the air was as thick as that.

"Charlotte," he said. Saying her name put him off balance. He slipped away from me, then stumbled back against my shoulder as we walked. I held him straight for a moment, like I was balancing a doll strung at the joints with rubber bands.

"You cursed me on the street," I said. "It wasn't long after I came to Charlotte."

"I don't remember. I believe you, though. I was crazy back then, that's the truth. But I'm sober now."

"For how long?" I asked him.

"Going on a year. When the year's up, Nellie says she'll join up with me for good."

I stopped on the path and stepped away from him into the wet grass. It licked at my ankles. "Who's Nellie? That woman on Mill Street?" I'd followed him there once after Mama died. There'd been a woman sitting on the porch in a broken down chair with ragged underwear on a line strung above her head.

"You knew about her?"

"I saw her. I wanted a mother so bad, I went down there to see if she would do. She wasn't anything like Mama."

"Lord God, she won't. Nobody's like my Hatsy." He was about to cry. "There ain't been nothing right for me since your mama."

I took his arm again. "You've kept a job?"

"I've lost more than I kept," he said. "People don't have infinite patience."

"And Nellie? Where'd you find her?"

"It was more her finding me, I think you could say. I wasn't looking to quit drinking, that's for dang sure, but one day walking home, there she was standing in front of me. Right there on the sidewalk in front of her house where I used to pass regular. She says, 'You look like a man in need of a boiled dinner,' and before I knowed what was what, I was sitting at her table looking at this feast she laid out and her scurrying around, chipping ice and all.

"I remember she opened a new jar of sweet pepper relish and poured me a quart of sweet tea. Lord, I wished it was a shot of whiskey! I tell you the truth, girl, I wanted a drink so bad my toes were curled up to my shoetops and the hair on my head was hurting. She knowed it, too, because she looks at me hard and says, 'You are a scrawny man if I ever seen one but I intend to fatten you up'." He laughed then, his head cocked to one side.

For a moment, he was like I remembered him. "I don't see that she's fattened you up much," I said.

"Well, I'm sober and I eat regular." He gripped my hand. "I'm forty-five years old and I reckon I look seventy. I've been no account most of my life."

I knew he wanted something from me but I didn't know what.

"I want you to come to the wedding," he said. When I didn't answer, he went on: "I want you to meet Nellie and see for yourself how things are going to be." He paused, sucking in his breath. I pulled my hand free from his. "If you don't like what you see, that can be the end of it. I know you've got a life here. I'm not blind to that."

"I don't know if I can, you know, start it up again," I said. "I loved you so much, Daddy, but I had to let it go."

We walked on a few steps, then I stopped and turned back. He knew not to come with me.

"So Charlotte's right," he said. "You're her child now."

"I don't see as I truly belong anywhere," I said.

Back at Charlotte's, the house was quiet. The children and Mac were asleep, so Charlotte and I sat in the dark kitchen that smelled of fried chicken and supper scraps. The dishes were still piled on the counter.

"If there's a wedding, I'll go to it," I said to her.

"I should do something about this mess," she said, looking at the dirty dishes instead of at me. "I can't stand a dirty kitchen in the morning."

"It won't mean anything, Charlotte," I said. "I just think it's something I should do."

"Once he tried to panhandle Mac on the street. That's how low he'll stoop," she said. "Then there was that time years ago when he yelled at you in front of Broydan's Store. Called you a bitch. Sloshed liquor down your coat before I could stop him. He wrote you letters, too. The most disgusting trash I've ever read. All about how he wanted you back with him, how he'd give you everything. It was lies, every word of it. I couldn't let him hurt you like that so I burned them. I'm not sorry."

"I'm grown now. I can decide," I said.

"Fifteen is not grown."

"I'm going to the wedding, Charlotte. You can't stop me."

"I know that." She got up then and pulled the light chain above our heads. We ducked, shielding our eyes, then faced each other under the light. She looked exhausted. Her dress was stained with perspiration and her face was shiny. Her mouth quivered. "Now you go on to bed. I'm going to do the dishes."

"I'll help."

"No, I want to do it myself."

So I left her there.

I waited to hear but there was no wedding, no plump, smiling bride coming up Charlotte's front walk to be welcomed into the family. Later that summer Mac told me he'd heard that Daddy was drinking again. I didn't try to find him. By then I was too much in love to go looking.

All We Know of Heaven

CHAPTER FIVE

 JOEL

I'd been intending to see her but not that way — when all I'd done was dip my head in the back porch basin and give it a quick rub. Everywhere else I was dirty as a tater from topping tobacco and loading fertilizer on the truck. Sweaty, too, it being a scorcher and all.

I would of missed her altogether if I hadn't been fooling with Daddy's biddies but I went on to the post office first like he told me to. He had fifty leghorns waiting, plus the nitrogen that had come in on the train.

When I got to the post office, Miss Trudy was in a swivet. Somehow those chicks had got loose and they were running all around, cheeping and carrying on. I went back there behind the counter and helped her get them in the box. Then on the way to the truck, I saw a little old black snake, as narrow as a pencil and about a foot long, slip between Miss Trudy's collard plants beside the post office so I put down the biddies and stuck it in my pocket. After that, I went on to the depot, backed up to the woodrack and slung the fertilizer bags on the truckbed.

That's how I come to be standing next to her at the station

window when the 11:42 blew down at the first crossing. She looked aggravated, like she'd had words with the station master before I got there. I could tell she didn't remember me from the hogkilling but I couldn't think how to remind her. Didn't see that it would be to my advantage anyhow, considering how I looked and smelled like a fieldhand.

When Mr. Stox slid my receipt under the grid, I had to lean past her to take it. I thought she'd look at me then but she didn't. She turned the other way, toward the open side of the depot and the tracks. I said to myself, you're going to let her get away again. So I followed her, but not real close. We waited a minute on the platform, listening to the train pass Devin's Crossroads where the whistle was sharp and full of warning.

"Expecting something?" I asked her and she looked me full in the face. Little beads of sweat was lying there on her throat and above her lip while I rested my hand on the snake's dry coil in my pocket.

"Some material. Charlotte's making us dresses for home-coming at Shiloh and they promised to send the material by Monday." Like she talked to me everyday. "If it's not on this train, she'll be fit to be tied," she said.

Cloth for dresses. Well, I didn't know what to say about that so I stared at the track and listened to the train coming. It bore down like it wasn't planning to stop.

"I can give you a ride home," I said just before the train slid out of a steamy cloud beside us. I couldn't tell if she heard but I kept on waiting till she got her package.

When she had it under her arm, I said, "I meant that about the ride. See, here's the truck right here."

She didn't hesitate a second. "All right then," she said and before I could get there, she pulled the door open and swung her-self inside.

The truck smelled like oil and fertilizer. The biddies were raising all kinds of racket in the box at her feet. I told her I'd put them in the back but she said never mind.

"I bet they're hot enough to roast though." She wiped her

finger across her lip like I wanted to do.

I started the truck. I couldn't believe we were talking so easy. The breeze our moving made was hot, then it cooled a little. I wished the Woodard's house was on the other side of the world. When we turned the corner harder than I meant to, she had to lean toward the window to keep her balance.

"What is that?"

Well, the snake had slid out of my pocket on the turn and before I could shift gears and get it, it was lifting its head and licking its tongue in the air. I shoved it back in my pocket, quick as a minute. She had a little knotted look on her face so I knew she was disgusted but what the hell, I went on and told her I was taking it home for the garden.

"Well, you must like snakes," she said. There was a little smile in her voice. I heard it.

I could feel my own self start to smile. "I don't want to get friendly with a cottonmouth but this here is just a little ole black snake."

"I know that but I still don't want one in my pocket." She was smiling to beat the band.

I pulled the truck over against the ditch in front of the Woodard's but left it running. Sunshine glared on the hood so bright I could hardly see out. I glanced over at her. She was staying, never mind how sticky hot she got.

"Summer's just getting started good," I said.

She nodded at me.

"It's going to be busy from now on."

The biddies were carrying on in their box.

"Course, there's Saturday afternoon and evening."

She nodded again. I felt like she was waiting for me to say something particular, something she already knew but still expected to hear.

"I want to come see you," I said as quick as I could. My face and neck were feeling scratchy, like the mat itch. "We could go to the show. Sometimes Ed and me go to Wilson's Beach. Do you ever go down there? There's a band on Saturday nights and on a hot day the river's nice and cool to swim in. Maybe they wouldn't let you go there, but there's the show —" I'd already said that. I was so hot and smelled so rank, I thought I'd burn up right there in front of her. Spontaneous combustion or whatever it was.

"Come sit on the porch one night," she said. The words came quick, like we were rushing toward something cool. "Come Saturday night after supper." She pushed the door latch and stepped on the running board, then jumped across the little ditch into the grass.

"I will," I said.

She nodded and started up the walk to the house. I just sat there and watched how her body moved under her dress. That black hair looked like a soft tassel dancing down her back. I couldn't move. It was like I was locked up. Hog-tied. Like that. Then she was inside and I was free.

I raced the engine, backing up. The biddies squeaked and scratched, trying to take hold. All the way home, I could hear her talking.

🌹 BETHANY

I couldn't decide what to put on. What do you wear to sit on the porch in the hot summertime? I didn't want to look like I expected to go somewhere. I tried on every dress in my closet — every time Mena passed my room, I was wearing a different one. There was something wrong with all of them but finally we settled on last year's Sunday best. It was blue with a white collar and a little lace box at the V. It fitted good in the waist and had those soft butterfly sleeves to help me stay cool.

After deciding on the dress, I squeezed six lemons for lemonade and opened a tin of nutty fingers Charlotte had been saving for a special occasion. I didn't even ask her.

The rest of the afternoon I sat in the swing stewing over what a nincompoop I'd been at the depot, going on about dresses when I know men don't care a fig about things like that. I'd looked terrible, too — a piece of twine holding back my hair and my old yellow dress limp as a rag.

He'd smelled bad himself, a working man's smell that could take your breath. I hoped I hadn't curled my nose or looked disgusted which was not my intention. What I planned to do was talk to him. I would say yes, yes, yes to whatever he asked. That's what I'd promised myself.

At supper I said, "You all don't come on the porch."

Charlotte looked mischievious. All day I'd avoided her so I wouldn't get teased. "I can't keep the children off their own front porch," she said.

"Mac, make them stay inside," I begged.

But he just grinned.

"Tell us who it is," Charlotte said. "We'll know in a little while anyway because I certainly do hope I'm not forbidden to look out the window."

"I know," Davey said. "I heard her talking to Olivia about him."

"You listened! Charlotte, he was eavesdropping!"

"Well, thank goodness!" Charlotte said. "Tell us who it is, sweetheart."

"It's Joel Calder," Davey said. "You told Olivia he gave you a ride home from the depot and he had a snake in his pocket. It crawled out on the seat and like to scared the daylights out of you!"

"A snake!" Charlotte was frowning. "What kind of person carries a snake around in his pocket?"

"Maybe he'll bring it tonight," Patsy said. "If he does, I want to see it."

"You will not!" Charlotte said. "I don't want you anywhere near a snake or him either, for that matter. He's —"

Mac said "Charlotte — "

But she went ahead. "Well, Mac, it's the truth."

My supper was churning in my stomach. All I could think about was that he'd be at the door in a few minutes. I wished I hadn't come to the table at all.

"I still want to see the snake," Patsy said.

"Mac, please! Make everybody stay inside!" I pleaded.

Nobody would promise, so when I saw his brother's little Austin pull up and Joel jump out and the car speed off again, I hurried to the porch before Mac could put down his paper or Charlotte dry her hands in the kitchen. Patsy came right behind me.

"Hello," I said and put out my hand like I was meeting him for the first time. Instead of shaking it, he cradled my fingers and I didn't pull away. I led him to the swing at the far end of the porch. After we sat down, my hand stayed in his.

"Hey, Joel, you got the snake?" Patsy asked him.

"Nope. It's home in the bean patch," Joel said.

She slipped onto the seat beside him. "Mama hates snakes. She won't even have one in the garden."

"You go back in the house," I said but she didn't budge. "Go on now and leave us alone."

"Patsy!" Mac called from the parlor. "You come in now!"

She poked her lip out at me and banged the screen door behind her. We sat there a minute, smelling the honeysuckle that was taking over the porch rail.

"I can't stay long," he said.

"I made lemonade for us to drink," I said. My hand slipped out of his. "Maybe I'll go get it."

"No, let's wait a little while," he said, taking my hand again just as naturally as picking up a book or a fork, like it belonged to him. "I'll be here from now on. I'm finished with school."

"I have one more year, then college."

"You want that?"

"Charlotte went to college. She was a teacher before she got married."

He pushed the swing with his foot and it moved slowly. The chain squeaked a little.

"I'm going to help Daddy out awhile. Then maybe I'll go

to Baltimore and find something there."

Neither of us said anything about there not being any jobs. It was like all of a sudden the Depression was happening some-place else and we had lots of possibilities.

Gradually the evening darkened around us and I went in to get the lemonade and cookies. The cookie he ate left a rim of sugar on his lip but I didn't know how to tell him.

He drained his glass. "I've got to be going, but I want to come again. Is that all right?" he asked. "Maybe if I can get Ed's car, we can go somewhere."

"Come for supper next Saturday," I said and it was decided.

🌺 CHARLOTTE

Since she'd already invited him, there wasn't much I could do except wash my hands of it which I did. Turned it all over to her — the menu, setting the table and arranging flowers, even ironing the napkins so slick they'd slide right off your mouth. Of course, it was time she had experience entertaining but I'd always thought it would be somebody like Douglas Watson, somebody at least social — certainly not the likes of Joel Calder.

There'd been stories about him for years. Of course, the Calders kept to themselves so who could know the truth of it but Mildred Howard told me herself how once in the sixth grade he put back his hand to hit her when she got after him about some kind of mischief — I don't know what. He didn't strike though. Maybe he scared himself out of it. Still the fact is he raised his hand.

"How about chicken salad?" Bethany was in the kitchen with Mena and me.

"Fine," I said but Mena eyed me over the canning jar she was drying.

"Law, you don't want to go givin that big strappin boy no salat," she said. "Give him roast beef or fry him up some chicken.

49

Satisfy him."

"Well, I'm not having the oven on all afternoon roasting a beef for anybody," I said.

"Fried chicken then." Bethany wrote it down.

"Rice with some good milk gravy and crowder peas," Mena said. "Now that be fittin for a man. Tomatoes. Biscuits. A peach shortcake."

I told Bethany she'd have to go down to Mr. Willis' herself and see if he had a mess of peas. "You'll have to shell every last one of them, too," I said.

"I will," she told me. "I'll do everything."

It scared me to see it was true.

🌹 MENA

Charlotte Woodard was a ornery woman — still is, not that she ain't mellowed some. Livin can do that to you. It beats on you sometimes, even white folks. I's seen her low.

Mad, too, and squawkin like a wet hen. I's in remembrance of another party, that time when I won't goin come help her. Well, I told her bout quarterly meetin weeks before time but she don't pay no nevermind. Time come and she go blamin me cause it ain't on her calendar in the kitchen. I been doin what needs doin in that house for years, but I don't write nothin down. No sirree! I could, but I don't. That be her business.

Anyways, I won't bout to miss quarterly meetin so she got to do that party all by herself, cookin, fixin, and all. I ain't sayin her hands won't full but don't nothin stand tween me and Jesus. Not even Miss Charlotte.

She fired me, too. First tries her sweet talk and all, wants to give me a dress — that blue one with the bias skirt and cummerbund belt. But I won't. So she gets mad and starts in on how I ain't suppose to come back. I's there on Monday anyhow. Go right on and starts gatherin up the wash and her standin in the kitchen like a rock. She done gone and hired that little ole Hazen gal, ain't but thirteen and lazy, too. That chile can't do no wash!

Bethany come upstairs after me, wantin to hear all bout meetin and the lady preacher there. I don't tell her a word, I so sick and shakin like a leaf. Emmaline's boy Simon was dead! He passed the night before but I still needs that dollar so I be standin there wrestlin with white folks' stinkin clothes and seein his little gray face and foamin mouth. He passed on the way to the doctor. In the wagon because Mr. George Malone won't take him in the car. "It can wait till mornin," Mr. George say. Like he's God Almighty.

I tells Bethany that, how that sweet baby bent double like a feed sack in the back of the wagon and passed.

"You ought to tell Charlotte," she say, tryin to hug on me but I won't bout to let her.

"And have her do what? Cry and moan how her kinfolk don't mean nothin by it?"

"Well, I don't reckon he did," Bethany says to me.

"It's a little niggerboy what don't mean nothin," I tells her. "His mama love him just like yours love you. His daddy use to hold him just like your daddy did you."

"I hate them," she says.

I remember what I told her clear as day. "Them Malones? No, you don't hate em. You one of em, girl."

She let me be then. All week she hung her head down low. When you prick her, she bleed.

CHARLOTTE

By six o'clock that evening Bethany had the table set and the meal cooked, she'd taken a sponge bath and put up her hair although the curls were easing out by the time she came downstairs to the door. She was wearing her pink flowered sundress and those white Sunday shoes she always said pinched.

We all followed her to the door and there he was, wearing what looked like somebody else's clothes, probably his brother's since he'd just been out of military school a few weeks. The blue jacket was a size too small and he had on a straw hat, straight-brimmed across his forehead which he didn't take off right away like he should have. A wolf in sheep's clothing, I thought to myself while Bethany put out her hand to him. The way he took it told me he had touched her before. The sack of blackberries he was carrying he handed to me.

Mac said, "Come on in, son," and led him into the parlor. Bethany and the children followed, so I went back to the kitchen alone.

At supper, Davey and Patsy watched him, watched Bethany, too, because she was cutting her chicken meat off the bone.

"You can just pick it up," Mac said to Joel. "That's what we usually do."

I asked after his mama. He said she was fine when I know well enough she's been sickly for years. Peculiar, too. She never did join in things like other folks. Of course, the woman's had her share of sorrow — some of it was sitting at my table.

After that, Mac did most of the talking. It was about farming and business so Joel didn't have to do much more than say "yessir" now and then. Everybody ate but me. I felt too stirred up to swallow.

"Why don't you serve the shortcake?" I said to Bethany before they were hardly through. The children gobbled theirs down and left the table, then Mac went out on the porch to finish the paper.

"You go on with Mac, Charlotte," Bethany said to me. "I'll do the dishes."

"I'll help," Joel said.

I felt too tired to move. Besides, this was her doings from beginning to end. "I certainly hope you'll be careful with my china," I said.

"Of course we will." Bethany was smiling at me but I could

see the tightness in her jaw, a warning that I was to leave her be.

A while later when I crept down the hall to see what was going on, the sight of them stopped me. The kettle of scalding water was whistling and I watched him take it off the stove and pour it slowly on the rack of soapy plates and glasses she'd washed. They stood together in the steamy heat and then he put his hand to her cheek.

"You must be the prettiest girl in the world," I heard him say and she laughed deep, like a sigh. His head went down to hers and met the sigh with a kiss.

I backed away, still watching. It was like I knew what I'd see even with my eyes closed, so I might as well look. What I dreaded most was happening. Not that I didn't want Bethany to fall in love. To marry. Of course, I wanted that. But not now and not with him. She couldn't know the pain in him, none of us could, but I knew it was there. I could see it on him.

Then I saw her dripping hands come out of the dish water and hold first his shoulders, then the back of his head as she pulled his face closer to hers, pressing her mouth tight to his. I teared up but I couldn't stop looking. Through that stringent light, it was my sister I saw.

JOEL

The river was wide at Wilson's Beach. We got there before noontime and the haze still hadn't burned off good. I could hardly see the tree line on the other shore.

I put down the old bedspread I'd brought while she took off the dress she was wearing. Course, she had her suit on underneath but when her skirt slipped down I couldn't help but look. It was the cloth sliding I had to see. She shook the sand off the dress and folded it up real neat in a little bag she'd brought. Then she sat down next to me. The sun was coming through a little bit. It lay flat on the water. The mica in the sand was bright, too. She shaded her eyes with her hand.

"Charlotte's making grape jelly today," she said, like her mind was still at home. Then I knew she was telling me something different. Charlotte had tried to stop her.

"But I came," she said.

Behind us at the pavilion, Mr. Wilson and his folks were stoking the hotdog cooker and icing down drinks in the drink box. "Daddy had work for me too," I said. "I gave one of the colored boys a dime to do it."

"So we're both free awhile." She lay back on the spread with her hand still covering her eyes. I stretched out beside her.

One of the Wilson boys came by dragging a basket of trash and I watched him to keep from looking at her. Already I'd seen the shape of her bosom where it sank in her swimsuit. Her skin had tiny freckles on it. I let my fingers creep across the blanket toward her shoulder. Did she want to go swimming? I asked her.

"Let's wait a little while. Till we're really really hot." She moved closer to my hand like she knew without looking it was there, just waiting to touch her. Her skin was sun-warmed and I could smell flowers at her neck where her pulse was. I knew I could put my hand there if I wanted to but it seemed like it was too soon.

They were sweeping the pavilion and the broom scratched at the sandy floor.

"I missed you all week," I said to her. "Every day, all day."

I wanted to ask her if any boys besides me came to sit on her porch. I wanted to hear her say they never would again, but she didn't.

"We can't be together all the time," was what she said. "You've got work and Charlotte — I've got things to do, too."

My hand grazed her arm then. She didn't move so I let my fingers run across her slick swimsuit, up between her titties, then on up to her neck. "Every boy in Whitney wants you," I said, resting my hand on her jaw.

"They do not!" I could feel her throat move when she talked. Then she rolled away from me. "Besides, I don't like any of them." Her face was hidden in the blanket but I heard. "I like just you."

Her hair was spread out all over her shoulders and I gathered it together and rested my hand in the thick waves down her back.

"What?" I wanted to hear it again.

She lifted her head onto my shoulder and buried her face there. "I just like you. Just you." Then she kissed my throat so soft it was like a flutter. An angel kiss.

All afternoon she was like a porpoise. She could slip in and out of the water, go down and then come up farther away from me or close, almost in my arms. She had learned to swim from her daddy who took her to the quarry when she was little. I could see her as a little girl jumping off the quarry ledge into his arms. I don't think she was scared of anything.

At sunset, we ate hotdogs and Coca-Colas at a picnic table under a tree. While we ate, the strings of lights came on at the pavilion. Most of the folks with children had already gone home but more cars were pulling in, couples like us. We could hear the band setting up.

I told her we'd stay and dance.

"But Charlotte's expecting me," she said.

"It won't hurt anything," I said. What could Charlotte do? "It'll be our first dance together."

"One dance," Bethany said.

But holding her and feeling the breeze off the river on her neck, I didn't intend to ever let her go.

CHAPTER SIX

🌹 EMMA

Do you think I'd of come to the door if I'd known it was Charlotte Woodard? Not likely. But there she was on the front porch, big as day. It was the early afternoon, too, when any sensible person would be lying down, what with the heat and all. She was looking down at those weedy nasturtiums J.C. planted near the steps after I told him not to bother. The rockers were turned up, too, and the curtains closed. She knocked anyway.

Right off I told her J.C. and the boys weren't home. "I thought you were the new tenant come to the wrong door," I said to let her see the inconvenience. My hair was loose and I was wearing an old housedress I'd lost the belt to. Charlotte was all flowered up in voile and high heel shoes.

"Well, Emma, I'm sorry if I've come at a bad time." But she sailed past me into the hall and went on in the parlor. It was dark and cool in there. "I've been hoping I'd run into you in town, but then you don't get out much, do you? I'd love to be a homebody myself but seems like I always hear duty calling." She sat down on one of Mama's low Victorian chairs before I even invited her to. "I thought I should have a talk with you about the children. I'm sure you know your Joel is seeing my Bethany."

"Ed said that." I rolled up a shade to give a little light and sat down myself.

"Well, to be frank, Emma, they're worrying me some," Charlotte said. "Bethany's so young — too young to be courting heavy — and lately it seems like they're together all the time."

"I don't see how that can be," I told her. "He works every minute. J.C. sees to it. Both our boys are hardworking." Just looking at her made me tired. "I'm not up to having company —" I started saying but she was already off on a tangent.

"He's on my front porch every night of the week, or else they're going somewhere together. You're not there to see it, but I am."

I didn't have a word to say about that.

"Surely you must see they're just children —" She stopped but I knew she wasn't finished. She didn't seem to see I was sick. She was sitting straight up on the chair like she was making a talk at one of those ladies' clubs she belongs to. "I thought maybe now that he's finished school, he'd be going off somewhere to find a job, make something of himself. I know you want that for him."

"He's farming with J.C. and Ed. We're doing as good as anybody."

"Emma, everybody knows he's high-strung."

I knew she was talking about the years since the accident. Seemed like only J.C. and me could remember before. "He was the sweetest little boy in the world," I told her.

"I know you were trying to help him when you sent him off to military school. It's been known to straighten some boys out."

"Seems like it did that," I said. "He's respectful."

"But there's a darkness in him, Emma. Surely you see

that."

"I reckon he does the best he can. We've done what we could for him."

"I appreciate that and I hope you'll consider how I feel about Bethany," Charlotte said. "Mac and I rescued her from abandonment. We gave her everything and now — now I feel like I'm losing her."

"I don't see what I can do," I said. I got up, hoping to see her out. "I know you think you can make everything the way you want it — you've come up like that — but I know different."

"But he lives under your roof. He's your responsibility!" When she stood up, the flowers on her dress were shaking. She brought to mind a snake. I saw she was mad enough to strike.

"Charlotte." It was J.C. in the doorway and we both fell under his shadow. The clock ticking in the hall behind him seemed louder than usual.

"Hello, J.C.," Charlotte said. "I came to talk to Emma about Joel and Bethany."

"Oh, they're all right." J.C. looked at me. I reckon he wanted me to agree but I couldn't say a word. "They're just young-uns."

"That's what I've just been saying. They're too young to be courting like they are," Charlotte said. "I see what's happening. I see affection between them —" She stopped like it was too hurtful to imagine. "We want Bethany to go to college. We want her to have a good life."

"I'll see about it," J.C. said. He stirred out of the doorway to let her pass. "Now you best be going, Charlotte."

"I didn't want to have to come out here like this," she said at the front door.

"Well, you did it anyhow," I said.

I watched her go. She turned her car around in the yard and headed off toward town. Then I heard J.C. going out the back. I didn't mind being left alone. All I wanted was to lie down.

❧ JOEL

I was in the hall when Daddy told me. "Charlotte Woodard came" was all he had to say before I got this scared feeling. It made me all hot inside like fire was shooting up my backbone right to my skull. It started burning there, too, so all I could hear was fire crackling. I couldn't hear Daddy, just my brain popping and that damn clock. It was ticking loud and I was burning.

My hand came up, a hard fist, and struck out, not at Daddy but at the clock. I felt the pane break around my hand and the glass spill out. It showered us both like sparks flying. My hand was bleeding where shards of glass caught in it. I reached into the works and grabbed the weights to jerk them free. The brass pendulum banged against the cabinet and stopped. My head started to cool a little. It was five minutes to five.

Blood was spurting from my wrist where I'd slid my arm across the ragged edge of glass. The quiet surprised me. I remember thinking motion should have noise to it, like splashing water or a sizzling pan. Blood coated my hand like I'd just pulled the guts out of a rabbit. The smell was sweet and thick like something you'd eat.

"God almighty, son, you're going to bleed to death!" Daddy said. I watched him ripping off his shirt, heard the crunch of glass under his feet. The cloth soaked red before I even felt the pressure. "Ed!" Daddy was screaming. "Goddammit, where is everybody?"

Then Mama was there, staring at both of us. Her hands were knotted at her chest and her mouth trembled but she didn't move.

"Get Ed," Daddy said. "Hurry, Emma. He's cut bad."

"It's just a scratch, Mama." My voice wasn't mine. It came from somewhere else, light as a feather.

ED

He passed out in the truck. Was dead to the world while Doc Frazier stayed the bleeding and sewed him up. Then Doc picked slivers of glass from his arms and neck and one deep shard from his jaw before washing him with antiseptic and bandaging him up.

Later I drove home with him sleeping in Daddy's arms. In his room, we stripped him out of his bloody clothes and poured a dose of painkiller down his throat, then put him to bed.

"Go tell Bethany Newell there's been an accident," Daddy said. "Tell her he'll be all right but don't say more than you can help." He looked worn out.

"I'll think of something," I said.

It was after nine o'clock when I got there. Before I was out of the car good, Bethany came out of the dark on the porch. She had ahold of the porch railing with both hands and all that hair of hers was wild and loose around her face.

Driving to town, I planned to tell her the truth, how the Calder clock brought over from England by our great-great grandpa was smashed all over the hall. How Joel had done it.

Maybe I should of told her how he killed a puppy once. Well hell, children do things like that. Me, I've stomped baby mice under my boot. I've shot starlings trapped under the barn roof and destroyed nests in the woods. I've never turned away from brandings or castrations. Well, it's the way of the farm.

Or I reckon I could of told about that time he threw a pitchfork at a little colored boy. Pierced his cheek. It wasn't in anger or for punishment either, but just because he wanted to let go the pitchfork and see it strike something moving quick and unaware. For days afterward, the boy throbbed with fever, glassy-eyed and crazy. His face swelled up so bad Daddy took him to Doc Frazier who opened it up and cleaned out the mixture of leaves and homemade salve his mama had packed in it. It was a week before the pus ran clear and Doc could stitch him up. When the crops came in that year, Daddy took the doctor's bills out of the family's share and they moved on. Sometimes I see that boy in town, near grown now but I know him from that pink ropey scar across his black cheek like his skin is turned inside out.

I knew Joel would be scarred up himself. His arm and probably a jagged mark on his jaw where that deep shard had been. I would of said that but her face stopped me. She was pale but she looked bruised, too, and her eyes were dark and wet.

"He's all right." That's what I said. "He got cut on a piece of glass. It's deep and he bled a lot but he's going to be fine."

"I want to see him," she said.

"He's sleeping now."

"He's truly all right?"

When I nodded, she said, "I thought he didn't want to come. I thought he'd seen another girl, woke up this morning and wanted something — somebody else." She had a shaky little smile. When she brushed her hair back, it sprang up around her face again.

"It was nothing like that."

Maybe I should of told her Charlotte had come. Maybe I should have said "you and him won't ever work out, there's too much against it" but I didn't.

"Charlotte will take me out there. I'll go tomorrow. I love him," she said.

JOEL

I knew she'd try to come. No matter what Charlotte said or did, sooner or later she'd be wanting things the way they used to be. She didn't know any better.

I was stuck there in my room all wrapped up. My arm and hand felt hot and throbby at first, then the cut got to itching and aching so bad I wanted to tear the bandage off to get at it. I didn't though. Doc Frazier said to keep still and I did the best I could. So

I couldn't stop her coming.

That morning they'd started on the cotton in the field that rims the woods and the women were coming back from dinner. I was by the window watching them drag their empty sacks like they were already loaded.

She said she drove herself. "Charlotte was resting so I just took the keys! She's been making excuses for days! Oh, Joel!" She came close by the chair, so close I got the shakes but I held my face away. It was the bandaged cheek she saw and my wrapped-up arm and hand. She was about to touch me but maybe she was scared to. I could tell how nervous she was. Myself, I was shivery cold.

"I've been so worried!" she said, leaning in. Then she went to babbling. "That night! Oh, Lord, I thought you didn't want to see me! I thought I'd die from it! Then Ed came and told me! I was so upset and worried about you, but relieved, too! I mean, it wasn't that you didn't want to come!"

I was hearing the sound of the clock and then the quiet, how I'd stopped it. I was supposed to be at the Woodard's at five-thirty for supper but I'd stopped its ticking at five, like I thought five-thirty would never come. I would never hurt her, even if it meant I could never see her again. That's what I thought.

"You ought not be here," I said.

"But I had to see you!"

"Well, now you've seen. You can go on home now."

"I will not! What in the world are you talking about? We —"

"There's no we, Bethany. There never was."

"Why, I'm beginning to think you're delirious or something! You can't turn off feelings just like that." She waited a little for me to make up to her but I didn't. "I know! You're mad because I didn't come sooner. Well, I wanted to. It was Charlotte. You know what a pill she can be!"

The cotton field blurred below. My head was pounding. "I want you to go and don't come back."

She didn't move and I couldn't see how to make her.

"Go on outa here," I said.

"You don't feel good," she said. "You've lost a lot of blood and I know you're weak as water. When you're better, you'll see everything's fine."

"I mean it, Bethany. It's over between us."

"That's not true." There was crying in her voice. "I'll come every day from now on. I can tell you're not eating just when you need your strength the most. Well, it's hard all bandaged up like that! I'll help you. It'll be fun! You'll be well soon and everything will be like it used to be."

"No. Listen to me. I don't want you here. Not now. Not ever." I couldn't look at her. If I saw her face, I wouldn't be able to give her up. I'd have to touch her no matter what. I didn't move a muscle till I was sure she was gone.

CHAPTER SEVEN

 MENA

Law, the way they do! You'd think they ain't got the sense God give a chicken. It's the truth. That girl was lyin round all day long, it seem like. Everywhere I wants to get, there she be. I have to clean round her.

She be stretched out on the porch with her eyes shut and her hands folded like a dead somebody and all a sudden she say somethin like: "Remember when I was always wantin to go home with you?"

Lyin there thinkin about them old times, that's what she doin. Dwellin on it, if you ask me. I just keep on sweepin.

"I used to want skin like yours. I'd turn your hands over to see where they're pink. Remember?" She don't move a muscle. It truly put me in mind of a corpse, her laid out like that when she ought to been up and doin.

"You was a crazy actin girl back then," I tells her. "You actin crazy right now, if you ask me. What you lyin round here all the day for?" I push the glider with my knee. Make it jiggle good.

"Waiting." She stop the glider with her foot.

"Huh! For what? That boy? Well, that's a poor notion if I

ever heared one. You wants that boy back, you got to see to it. Go where he at if he ain't comin here."

Miss Charlotte come out then. She don't care nothin about how that chile actin.

"Here's your money," she say. She stand right there while I ties it up in a handkerchief and push it in that snug place between my bosoms. "You can go on home when you get finished sweeping," she say and sail in the house, haughty as you please. Miss Queen of the World, that's Charlotte Malone sure as day.

I leans on the broom. It be bout broke down anyhow. "Me and Watteau, we calls it quits one time, don't see eye to eye bout nothin. Him wantin to stay out there on Mr. Rowe's place, and me, I's aimin to get to town. I won't as old as you but I knowed my mind. I knowed what I wanted — Watteau and a house that won't facin the same ole sorry corn patch year after year. So I gives in a little, say all right, I'll stay out yonder. Got myself hitched as quick as a minute. Then I starts in on us movin off the place. Got that, too, when the time was right."

"Mac gave Watteau a job at the mill," Bethany say. "The first colored man to have a good paying job in town. Charlotte told me."

Now that get my dander up good. "Ain't you folks got nothin to do but talk bout colored folks?" The parlor clock starts in marking three and I sweeps a long, wide stroke. "Miss Charlotte been doin some big talkin to them Calder folks. Been out there sayin her mind. You can know that for the truth."

"She did what?" That girl get off the glider so fast it bang against the house loud enough to wake the dead. Her color come back, too.

"I heared her say to Miss Milly how she went."

"When, Mena?" She got me by the shoulders. By then she was full grown. Tall like me, and strong limbed.

"Before he got hisself hurt, I know cause Miss Charlotte say she don't care a thing bout that. Say all she after be fixin it so he don't come round here a-courtin you no more. She don't care how she done it."

"Oh, God! Oh, God." She be shakin like a leaf. Look mad and happy all at once. "It's not like he said at all! It was Charlotte!"

"Well, you just keep me clear of it," I tells her. "I don't hear nothin and I don't say nothin round here."

She go to huggin on me then. Like to squeezed the life out.

"You ain't plannin to take that car no more, is you? If you is, I don't want to hear bout that neither," I says.

"What can I do? What can I do?" She let go of me and start flittin around and mumblin like she tetched in the head. "Mac! I'll talk to him! I know he'll help me!"

That's how come she walk toward home with me. Went along far as the gin. She be like somebody what's been filled with the spirit. You all knows what that look like.

❀ MAC

Bethany had to come through the gate, then past the mill, the oil house and the gin before she got to the office. I've situated myself that way so men wanting to pass the time of day won't find it so convenient. I know what it's like — you stand around waiting to get your cotton weighed, watch it being ginned, too, if you can. You make sure you don't get short-changed a boll. The crop's about all you've got so I understand. But I've got business, too, and enough paperwork to keep me down there half the night. I don't stay late, though. I go home of an evening at a reasonable hour. Charlotte wouldn't have it any other way and neither would I. Otherwise, what's the point of having a family?

That said, I didn't mind stopping for Bethany who is like my own, not that she's always thought so. We were slow getting used to each other, if the truth be known. Charlotte kept getting in the way, taking on all the responsibility like she'll do if you don't fight her tooth and nail, but gradually Bethany and I got to mean something to each other even if Charlotte and I weren't her real folks. I could see how Harriet and Warren stayed alive in her mind. She remembered them.

"Well, how-you-do, young lady," I said when she came in that day all hot and bothered. "The last time I saw you, you were prostrate and intending to stay that way."

"I got up." She leaned on my desk and took a piece of hard candy from the jar I keep there. It was stuck together from the heat so she sucked on two.

"Well, I'm glad to see it. We've all got hurts behind and in front of us. We've just got to keep going." That's what happens when you finally get to have your say — you're bound to say too much.

She ruffled the cut edge of the ledger book I was working on. "It's not finished between Joel and me." She was so calm and matter-of-fact, it was hard to believe that yesterday she'd been moping and carrying on.

"Well now, honey, he said it was. At least, that's how you heard it."

"I was wrong."

"Bethany —"

But she stopped me. "I need to see him. Everything wasn't said." She was sucking on that candy like she could draw all the sweetness out at one time. "Charlotte won't help me. You know that."

Outside, a creaking wagon came to a halt with a solemn "whoa."

"The tobacco market opens tomorrow and I'll be going over there," I said after a little thought. "I don't suppose it would hurt for you to go along with me."

"And you think he'll be there?"

"I've never known a Calder to miss opening day. Every farmer drawing breath tries to be there."

"I'll go," Bethany said.

I slipped my visor down on my forehead. "You know, honey, people do things because they think they have to, because they think they're right. They act on true feelings of concern and still they hurt people."

She knew I was talking about Charlotte.

"She shouldn't have interfered," Bethany said.

"Well," I said, "I don't know that she did but if that's the case, it was out of love, and what I'm doing, it's coming from the same place."

She didn't hug me or anything. We didn't do that. But I remember how she looked at me. After she left, I felt blinded for a minute so I waited a little before going back to work.

🌸 BETHANY

He was running with a pack of boys when I found him. After what seemed like hours of walking up and down in front of warehouses and wandering through the crowds inside, I saw him ahead of me on the street. He had his shirt sleeves rolled up so I could see his bandaged arm. He didn't seem to favor it. The hoodlums he was with were hooting and hollering, making fun of country boys left to watch their loaded wagons. One of them dropped an empty bottle under the feet of a nervous mule who stamped and whinnied, making the wagon sway until the boy in charge could calm it.

I went along behind, keeping him in view. He was eating roasted peanuts and dropping the shells on the ground. The bandage on his cheek was gone but I wasn't close enough to see the scar.

When he and his gang turned into an alley between two warehouses, I waited for a minute at the entrance, trying to decide what to do. I didn't want to walk right up to him in the wrong place. I could see some shacks back there, old mill houses they looked like. I waited till they passed through the alleyway, then I went down it, too, and came out in the sunlight. As quick as I could, I stepped out of view under the shade of a chinaberry tree.

Joel was banging on the door of one of the houses. It finally opened and a girl came out on the porch. She was wearing a flimsy dress and she leaned one hip against the railing and slid her bare foot against her calf. Joel was standing next to her, close but not touching. He said something I couldn't hear and they both laughed and she put her hand on his chest like she was going to push him away but she didn't. She let her hand rest on his shirt while her other hand ran down his arm to the bandage. I shut my eyes.

I'd seen this before — a mill house with broken steps and puny flowers, a woman at the door, the smell of coal fires and meat boiling. I'd been a little girl hidden in the dust of a passing wagon, watching my daddy go in such a house. I'd seen the door close behind him.

I stepped out of the shade. "Joel," I said, surprised by my own voice, how it carried above the other boys' heads. It lifted over the complaining traffic and the cries of vendors and auctioneers working the tobacco sales.

He squinted out at me, then brushed past the girl on the porch so fast I hardly knew what to do. I started down the alley, thinking he'd follow me. That's what I thought — I'd call his name and he'd come. But he didn't. When I turned around, he was standing in the light at the end of the alleyway.

"Leave me be!" he yelled. I could see his clenched fists, his drawn up shoulders like his whole body was fighting against me. "I mean it! You keep away!"

But I didn't. I couldn't. Later that afternoon I found him again. He was coming out of the picture show and the brightness outside made him stop and shade his eyes while I caught up with him.

"I know what happened," I said.

"I don't know what you're talking about." He wouldn't look at me.

"I know about Charlotte. The clock. Everything." I had to hurry to keep up with him.

"Then you know I'm not going to see you anymore," he said.

"I know you love me." I stopped on the sidewalk and watched while he moved ahead of me almost at a run.

Near suppertime, I found Mac waiting in the truck and climbed in beside him.

"Well, did you find him?"

I nodded.

"What happened?"

"Nothing."

He started the engine and let it idle a moment. "I'm sorry, honey," he said.

"Don't be," I said although I couldn't say for certain what I meant.

The next evening I heard the truck rumble to a stop in front of the house and then a voice whispering my name. It floated around the deaf in the parlor — Mac with a book, Charlotte on the other side of the lamplight hemming a dress, Patsy making a puzzle on the rug. It moved down the wide hall into the kitchen where I'd just poured out the dishwater and was buffing the counter with a dry cloth. I stopped mid-wipe to hear my name. It stroked my ear and cheek, made tears spring. I dropped the cloth to follow the voice to the front door, past the parlor and Charlotte who concentrated completely on the whip stitches she was making.

"I love you," he said through the screen and I was in his arms before even one breath could pass between us.

CHAPTER EIGHT

CHARLOTTE

Well, I should have talked to Emma and J.C. differently, I see that now. I should have kept my wits about me better than I did. I know they've always been private people and the truth is we've all got family business we keep hidden as best we can.

"Harriet should of never married Warren Newell in the first place," I told Mama when I went out home to tell her all that had happened. We were on the front porch so I could look down through the trees toward Papa's store where Patsy had gone to get a bottled drink out of the cold box. Bethany was in the kitchen fixing us a cup of tea.

Mama fished her Tube Rose out of her pocket and ruffled the feathery edge of her snuff brush against her finger before softening it on her tongue. "Well, now," she said, "my memory is that Warren was a handsome man." She took a dip and put the can back in her pocket.

"I never could see it." The maples in the yard were beginning to turn and a red leaf caught my eye now and then.

"You didn't want to see it. You've always wanted your own way, Charlotte," Mama said in that soft tone of hers. She had a knack for saying the hardest things without getting a person riled. "Come sit, honey. You're wearing me out flitting around." Her rocker moaned when she leaned over to position the spittoon she kept beside the chair. "Do you think I didn't lie awake scared to death about all of you? Women do that. We think we can change what happens but now I know we can't. I couldn't. Maybe I failed Harriet letting her marry Warren, but I don't know as I could of stopped her — no more than you can stop Bethany now."

"Well, they're not married yet. There's still time."

"Time for what?" Bringing the tea tray, Bethany let the screen door bang behind her.

I looked at Mama but she'd leaned away to get rid of her dip.

"Charlotte's got something she wants to tell you, honey," she said after she'd wiped her mouth on her handkerchief.

Bethany rested the tray on Mama's little porch table and poured. "It's about Joel, isn't it? Oh, Mama Bess, I'm so crazy about him I can hardly stand it, but Charlotte hates him. I know she does."

"Do you talk to each other? Truly talk?" Mama asked her. "You and Joel, I mean."

"Of course we do!" Bethany leaned against the railing, looking at us like she could stop what might be coming with a stare. "We say everything!"

My cup and saucer were rattling on my lap. "Then of course you know what happened to his baby sister," I said.

"What about her?" Bethany asked me.

I could see she didn't even know there'd been a baby sister.

"Charlotte, you'll do anything to break us up! I'm not going to listen to you at all!"

"Well, J.C. and Emma did have another child, honey," Mama said. "Of course, what happened was an accident. No doubt in the world about that." She put her cup down carefully and I knew she was going to tell it. I don't know, maybe she didn't trust me with it. I waited.

"If I remember correctly, the boys had been out rabbit

hunting and they came in all cold and blustery, bragging about all they'd done and Joel — he was nine then, maybe ten — he puts his gun against the wall so he can empty his pockets and show his mama his rabbits. Doesn't put the safety on or empty the shells, not any of the things I know his daddy taught him. There's little Alice on a pallet in front of the stove — she's a year old if she's a day. I don't remember exactly." Mama glanced over at me but I was holding still.

Bethany looked like a ghost, as pale and untouchable as that.

Mama sighed and went on. "They were all right there in the kitchen and Joel picks up his gun, going to hang it up, I reckon, seeing how he's got his coat off and the rabbits spread out on paper. And that gun just goes off. Well now, he had to of touched the trigger — that's the only way it could of been — and in a second that poor little baby girl was dead. There wasn't a thing to be done."

"No!" Bethany said. The whole porch seemed to tremble. I watched the trees in the yard quiver on a cool breath of wind.

"It's the truth," I told her. "He's got this hurt every minute of his life and he hasn't seen fit to tell you about it." My arms ached to reach for her but I didn't. Let her feel it, I thought. Let her know the crush of it. "Not telling is the same as a lie," I said.

"He couldn't!" she cried. "Don't you see? He was afraid! Oh, he shouldn't have been! He should have known I'd love him no matter what — I'd love him more! Now I see how he needs me, Mama Bess. He truly does!"

"They sent him off to military school," I said. "They couldn't do a thing with him so they sent him off! He couldn't get along with anybody. He's a misfit! Can't you see that? He's going to break your heart!"

"You're the one hurting me, Charlotte!" Bethany cried. She dropped down beside Mama's knees. "Make her stop, Mama Bess! Make her!"

Patsy was coming up the lane. I watched her twirling her Coca-Cola bottle on her thumb.

"Why didn't you leave that bottle in the rack?" I yelled when she was close enough to hear. "Can't you do anything right?"

Then I stood there quaking while my child turned back down the dusty road, going away from me when what I really wanted was to hold her in my arms.

❧ MAC

"A chip about the size of a pinhead." That's how Charlotte described the engagement ring Joel gave Bethany at Christmas. "It takes a magnifying glass to see it," she said to anybody who'd listen although I know she talked more openly to Milly Holmes than she did to family. Pride got in the way with close relatives. Besides, Milly and Wilton's children were younger than Bethany and not to be compared.

My idea was to talk them into waiting a year, maybe even two. Hard times ought to be argument enough. Joel didn't have a job except working for his daddy and things were too tight at the mill for me to take him on there. No automobile, no house unless they fixed up a tenant shack out there on the Calder's place. I could use myself as an example, tell them how I was almost thirty before I had the financial security to take on a bride. Brought her straight to this house, too. Set her up with every modern convenience. I could say Bethany was used to luxury which was a fact. She was accustomed to the finest, at least by Whitney standards. And I had money for her education, too; could scrounge enough to put her through most any college if she'd just do it. She was smart enough. Was she going to let all those years of straight A's go down the drain?

"Well, don't say that," Charlotte fretted. "Let's just get her into a program — a two year teaching certificate over there at Lawrence College, a bookkeeping course, anything that will put off this marriage long enough for her to come to her senses."

What she really wanted was for me to let her do the talking. She didn't trust anybody. Look how the Calders had failed her. Mama Bess, too, for that matter.

"Married! And she's still a child!" She stalked around the house, making herself miserable. "Why, she's at the beginning of her life!"

"Tell her she can't," Milly advised her. "Tell her she'll have to run off and elope."

"For heaven's sake, she might do it!" Charlotte fumed.

Turned out, Bethany wanted a wedding. "After graduation," she said to Charlotte and me. She'd come in from being with him and I could tell she had just combed her hair and put on fresh lipstick. She was standing in front of the fire like she needed to get warm although she looked flushed in the face.

"I'll get a job and Joel can keep on with his daddy until something better comes along —"

"Which it never will," Charlotte said. "I know you're seeing this rosy future, Bethany, but however you start out, that's how you'll be stuck forever."

"What about your education?" I asked her. "I've got money for your college."

"Maybe we could have some of it to fix up a house. J.C. says there a place out there for us, if we're willing to work on it."

"No!" Charlotte said. "Not a penny for that! If you don't use that money for school, then it'll be Davey's. We're not going to see it frittered away on curtains and do-dads!"

"Well, the money doesn't matter anyway," Bethany said.

"Of course, it does! What did you ever want you didn't get, girl?" Charlotte said. "Why, you're talking about being a tenant wife like it's something to be proud of! Tenant wives go to the back door, Bethany. They work in the field or else do somebody's wash just like colored people!"

"It won't be like that! He'll be farming for his daddy! It's not the same!"

"Maybe not, but it can feel the same. You've got to own something if you're going to be somebody."

"I just want to be his wife." Bethany slumped on the stool beside my chair. "I just want to belong to somebody and have them belong to me, don't you understand that, Charlotte?"

"You belong to me." Charlotte's voice was so hard I slammed my book shut to stop her. She looked me in the eye then went on, more tenderly, it seemed to me. "You belong with our family, sweetheart. You're one of us."

"I know that," Bethany said. "But I must be with him, too. I have to be. I won't give him up again, not for anything."

The fire spit around a pine knot, then sent a licking flame up the chimney. We sat there watching the blaze leap and dance. Outside the March wind rattled the shutters and pushed against window panes. The nandina branches I never got trimmed made a racket against the house. Inside, the room was quiet. I looked at Charlotte who was bent forward, her head lowered toward the fire. She looked so helpless, like she was actually sick. I didn't see what I could do to help her.

🌺 CHARLOTTE

"Well, once he's had his way with her, he might not be so interested in getting married," Milly said. "Think about that, Charlotte." She was holding her hands under her round belly like she could already cradle the baby in there.

"And do what? I can't encourage her to sleep with him, for heaven's sake." Through the window, I could see Patsy tending Milly's three children. A soft wet snow had fallen that morning and she was helping them make snow balls.

"Well, it's the only thing I can think of," Milly said. "When Wilton was courting me, Mama went on night and day about falling into sin — she's about as bad as Wilton for preaching —and I tell you the truth, it made 'doing it' seem all the more inviting." She sighed. "Actually, when the time came I had to wonder what all the fuss was about." This from somebody who was carrying her fourth baby in eight years.

"Well, I don't think that will be the case with Bethany. Anyway, I can't risk it," I said. "I've been thinking about sending her off to Mac's sister in Richmond." The children were rolling in the snow and when they staggered up, their clothes looked sopping wet. I started to rap on the window to get them in but then I saw a pink haze through the smoky clouds to the east. The sun was coming out. The snow would be gone by noon.

Milly was talking behind me. "She wouldn't go off to Richmond. Why, you'd have to gag and tie her! And what about high school? You can't send her off before graduation."

"I could go find Warren. That's the only thing left. I could tell him he has to stop her."

"He wouldn't do it!" Milly said. "What has he ever done but neglect her?"

"Charlotte!" It was Bethany in the hall. She came in red-cheeked, bringing cold on her coat and the knit cap she flung on a chair. Olivia was behind her and they leaned against the stove, collecting warmth on their hands and faces. "I showed Olivia the house," she said. "She loves it."

Olivia gave me a sly smile. I've never thought that highly of the Washburns but Olivia has been a good friend to Bethany. She said, "I didn't say that exactly. I said it would do if you can stop the wind blowing through the cracks and the snow coming in under the roof. There's a drift a foot high in the kitchen."

"There is not!" Bethany was getting a pot for making chocolate and she slapped it on the stove with a bang. "A little flurry in one corner, that's all. And J.C. promised us a new roof."

"And paint, I hope. And a new porch railing and some linoleum to cover up those terrible floors," I added.

"I didn't know you'd been out there." Bethany was measuring cocoa and sugar into the milk while Olivia stirred.

"Well, I have and it hurts me to the core to think about you living like that when you could stay right here and take a business course, you could go to any college you want to, you could go with Olivia wherever it is she's going. You've got all these options —"

"Charlotte," Milly said, "maybe she doesn't want —"

But I wouldn't let Milly interfere. "You're throwing yourself away on the first hot hand that comes along. You've got to resist it! It's not Joel Calder, it's — it's —"

"Sex!" Milly was patting her bulging middle like she was there to provide evidence.

"I love him," Bethany said and hit the measuring cup against the pot so hard it tipped over, spilling milk into the jet. It sputtered and flamed higher. The scorched smell filled the kitchen.

"Well, don't just stand there, clean it up." I pushed between them to put out the flame. Bethany was standing beside me while Olivia worked with a damp rag, sponging up the milk.

"I love him," she said, quietly this time. We were closer than we'd been in a long time, shoulder to shoulder with the heat off the stove on our faces.

"I know you do," I said. It was true whether I liked it or not.

CHAPTER NINE

 JOEL

I did everything I was told — worked like a dog shrubbing ditches. Cut stalks, disked fields, slung manure off the wagon into the furrows. The stench hung on me and by night my clothes could stand on their own from the dirt and sweat. On week nights, I stayed away from the Woodards. Maybe I'd go out to Hamm's to play poker and have a few beers. Now and again I went to Lawrence and messed around the pool hall but damn, all the time she was on my mind.

Most nights I stayed home. I kept a pint in my room and I'd lie there in the dark sipping and listening to the countryside. She seemed so far away then. Might as well been in Timbuctoo.

Of course, we spent the weekends together, starting with the Friday night basketball game. She was their best forward, tall and quick like she was. Her hair danced down her back and she looked damp all over. Slick. God, she was beautiful.

We'd hold hands under our coats during the boys' game, then head back to Charlotte's to eat the leftovers from supper. Sometimes I'd put a dollop of whiskey in my coffee — Bethany showed me where Mac kept it under the sink behind the Gold

Dust. About midnight we'd hear Charlotte's slippers flopping down the hall. "Oh, you're still up," she'd say like we'd surprised her.

I knew to say good-night then. The house was dark before I got off the porch good.

On Saturdays we worked on the house. By April Daddy and I had a new tin roof on and a pine porch rail. Bethany fixed up inside. She stripped the layers of newspaper off the front room and bedroom walls and covered them with flowered wallpaper left over from Charlotte re-doing her dining room. We painted the kitchen the color of cream and scrubbed the linoleum floor and cleaned the wood cookstove till it shined.

"Do you think you can cook on it?" I asked her.

"Of course I can!"

That's what she said about using the pump on the back-porch, the tin bathtub hanging on a nail out there, the outhouse a few yards away. "Yes," she kept saying. Yes to everything.

We put a sink in the kitchen and Daddy ran an electric wire down from the house and put a light socket in every room. Mama came down one day with some oil lamps she'd cleaned up but she wouldn't come in and look. Bethany's Uncle George came in his truck with an old oak breakfront, a table and four chairs Mama Bess was giving us. Mac came, too — brought a new store-bought bedstead Charlotte didn't know about. "You don't tell her, either," he warned us. He was grinning. "I want the pleasure myself."

Sometimes we stayed at the house until past dark of a Saturday. We'd skip the picture show or whatever doings Ed knew about. We'd even miss Charlotte's supper. We'd lie in the dark on the bed Mac had brought and fumble around under our clothes until Bethany would jump up all a sudden and fix herself as best she could with no mirror to see in. She'd smooth her tangled hair with her hands. They would flutter like little birds around her face.

"Take me home!" she'd say in the dark. "Before it's too late, Joel, take me home!" And I would.

🌷 CHARLOTTE

The week of the wedding, I found Sister's china in the attic exactly where I'd put it all those years before. I could hardly believe I hadn't repacked it in all that time but there it was, still in that old cardboard box I'd brought it home in. Silverfish had been at the glue so I opened it right there in the attic, naturally expecting to find broken pieces. There wasn't a chip anywhere.

Looking at one of Hatsy's plates, I could see Bethany as clear as day coming across the yard to the car with that old satchel in her hand. I remembered her defiant stare when she was about to refuse whatever I wanted for her — dresses, ballet lessons, piano practice, patent leather shoes, even school. No wonder I hadn't given a thought to dishes. There wasn't time to think about china with Bethany to contend with. I had my mind on LIFE all those years.

I stood up, cradling the box in my arms, and looked down the disappearing staircase. The china was shifting in the flimsy box. To tell the truth, I didn't think I could do it.

"Mac!"

He appeared below and took one step on the shaky stair. "What are you doing up there?"

"Here, take this." I handed him the carton, then sat down on the attic floor, my feet on the first rung. It was already warm up there and I felt like I couldn't get a good breath. I bent over, my face almost in my lap, trying not to cry.

"What is it, Charlotte?" Mac reached up for me. "Come on down, honey."

I didn't want him to see me carrying on. I've hardly ever cried in my adult life. What good does it do to blubber and moan, to be blinded like that? I've always wanted to see clearly. I've wanted to be ready for whatever needed doing.

"Charlotte, come on down, honey. I don't think this ladder will hold both of us."

"I'm all right." I wiped my face with the back of my hand.

"Here." He was reaching up with his handkerchief and I took it. "Charlotte, you've got to just let this happen because there's no stopping them. You've done everything you could do."

"And here I am giving them a reception." I managed a little smile. "I'm making them a wedding cake."

"It's all going to work itself out." Mac held out his hand and I took it.

"I want to believe that so bad," I said, coming down. But in my heart, I didn't.

🌿 EMMA

I made myself a dress. J.C. took me all the way to Lawrence to get the material. It was rose colored and slipped under my needle so I had to sew real slow to make it turn out fit to wear. I used an old pattern with a high neck and long sleeves but I decorated it some with a band of lace around the cuffs and collar and two rows down the bodice. It was nothing like what Charlotte Woodard would wear — I knew that. She'd be wearing silk stockings and fancy jewelry, too. I knew what to expect from her.

What surprised me was Joel getting married before Ed and in a church, too. We are not the church-going kind although J.C. and me were both brought up that way. After my baby died, the preacher at Devin's Crossroads Methodist used to come all the way over here to see me but finally he gave up. I wouldn't talk to him, that's a fact.

For the longest time, it was like I didn't notice anybody, not even my own. I scrubbed the boys' clothes, changed their beds, passed food to them at the table but I didn't see them. I didn't want to. I noticed J. C., of course. Sometimes lying there next to him, I'd remember when we were young and expected life to treat us good or at least fairly. Well, there wasn't much fair in it that I could see and so mostly I turned my back on him, too.

The note from Charlotte said the wedding would be at Shiloh Church at one o'clock followed by a reception at the Woodard home, 116 Coleridge Street, like we didn't know where the house was. I knew I'd go, too. And hold my head up. I'd show a different side from the one Charlotte saw when she came busting in here, wanting none of this to ever happen.

You can't stop everything. That's what I wished I'd said to her. I couldn't stop the bleeding that left me barren. I couldn't keep my baby from dying like she did. I couldn't stop my boy from closing up his grief inside.

Maybe he was dark inside like Charlotte said. Even crazy. Maybe we all were, thinking we could slip through the knots of life and get free. I just thought Joel deserved a chance at it and I made myself a new dress to prove it.

"What are you doing?" J.C. had caught me standing there in front of the mirror in my old cotton slip, the dress around my ankles. I stepped out of it quick and grabbed my housedress to my chest.

"I just tried on the dress," I told him.

"I reckon I'll just brush up my winter suit and hope the weather stands with me," he said.

"I could of done without the dress," I said. In the mirror I could see my pinched face and stringy neck. My shoulders looked bony and stiff.

"No," he said and came into the reflection I was looking at. "You can look as pretty as the next woman, Emma, if you've a mind to."

I shook my head and started to put my housedress on.

"Wait a minute," my husband said. His fingers were thick and calloused and lay heavy on me. "Let me look at you."

To keep him from it, I went into his arms.

🌺 BETHANY

When I hugged Charlotte good-bye, it was like hugging a board. I'd already passed through the entire house, starting with the kitchen where Aunt Lucille was washing stacks of punch cups while Lizzie scraped frosting off the cake plate. Milly was drying glass plates best left to air dry. Mena was there too. She had that disgusted expression behind her eyes like she wished they'd just go on home and leave it all to her. She was going to have to clean up after them anyway because Aunt Lucille was sloshing sink water over the side like she was in the washhouse and the plates were coming out streaky.

Then I went to the parlor where Mac and the other men had shed their suitcoats and were slumped in chairs, smoking and sipping whiskey Mac had brought out at the last minute. Mama Bess and Papa Rowe I found on the porch, out of the afternoon sun but where they could keep an eye on Milly's children who were apt to push the tree swing too high or run in the road without looking.

Joel was in the truck with the motor running — that's how fired up he was — or maybe it was plain old boredom because we hadn't been at the reception fifteen minutes, hardly got the cake cut, when he was after me to get going. I wouldn't, though. It felt like it was the last time I'd ever be my old self — I didn't feel married yet — and I guess I wanted to stay a girl a little while longer.

Not that I regretted anything. My wedding was as pretty as a picture and I meant every word I pledged. So did Joel. At the vows, he spoke up clearly when I half expected him to mumble. He looked so handsome, too. There's never been a better looking man in the world than him.

Charlotte was in the upstairs hall when I found her, Joel with the motor running in the yard, the children squealing, women talking and clattering dishes in the kitchen. She was separate from it all, like she'd suddenly had a spell of loneliness right there amid all the goings-on.

"Joel's waiting," I said.

"Then you best be going," she said and sniffed hard. She had put on fresh lipstick and powdered her nose.

"Well, let me hug you," I said and wrapped my arms around her. It was the first time I ever really noticed that I had grown up to be bigger than she was.

🌺 JOEL

I drove all night with her asleep against my shoulder and her hand curled palm up on my thigh like she was too tired to hold on. The road swayed in front of us and sometimes I just about dozed but I always caught myself in the nick of time. We couldn't afford to stop until we got to Chimney Rock and Heaven's View Motor Court where we'd already sent a deposit. I wasn't about to do anything in the bed of the truck. Didn't seem right to even consider it.

Then when we got to the place, we had to wait two hours for them to get the room ready. Once we got in it — a frilly pink room they called the bridal suite — we were too wore out to move and went right to sleep with our clothes on. We woke up late in the afternoon starving and went over to the restaurant where they had chicken and dumplings for the supper special.

I can't say much about how it was from then on. I know this: my hands found every warm place — the wet tangled curls around her ears, the sticky hair under her arms, the thin line of damp under her bosom and behind her knees. I wanted to talk to her, tell her how sweet she was, how everything I'd ever wanted or needed in my life was right there, I was kneeling over it. But I couldn't say anything. I didn't know the right words for what I felt for her.

🌹 BETHANY

Later on, we slept. That was the strangest part, that we didn't have to get up and go home. Charlotte wasn't waiting and we weren't listening for Ed's car horn. Everybody said it was going to hurt but it didn't. Maybe a girl can be that ready, so ready nothing can hurt her even if he comes with a fury which he did, slamming in me till the bed shook and I was trembling weak.

Then we slept. When I woke up the room was dark and I slipped into the bathroom to wash myself. In the dim light, I looked bruised. I was cold, too, and there was a new tenderness between my legs. I went back to bed and pulled the covers over us. Joel was sleeping on his back, his body spread out like there was nobody in the bed but him so I curled on my side right on the edge. I waited a while, trying to go back to sleep but I couldn't. Toward dawn, I put my arms around him and he came out of sleep like a child full of sighs that washed across my neck. Without a word, he moved over me, his slow, heavy breath making a shivery breeze on my belly. That time when he lifted me up against him, I felt like I was an instrument he could play. I was all strings and the sound I made whispered in the room.

CHAPTER TEN

🌹 BETHANY

Dear Olivia,

It is autumn here. Suddenly today it came, bringing the bluest sky I've ever seen without a single cloud but a gusty wind that rattles the leaves on the sweetgums and sends the fallen ones blowing everywhere. I have swept the kitchen porch twice this morning because it is low to the ground and the leaves skitter across it and dance right in the door every time I open it.

My new kitten Amos is after them every minute until he is so tired he just falls down asleep. He must think the sky is full of moths and butterflies because he sees the leaves as living things he has to pounce on if he is to grow into a respectable cat. Now he is just a little yellow mound of fur curled here at my feet with his white face hidden. I hope he turns out to be a good mouser but not too much of a tom. Joel is all the tom-cat I can handle!!!

I am working at the bank. Ours is the only one in the county still open. Mac and Mr. Watson went around saying how if everybody would leave their money in, it wouldn't have to close. People did that so now I stand in my little cage all day and handle money. It is old and wrinkled and by the end of the day I feel dirty from it.

Joel picks me up in the truck every afternoon at five except on Thursdays when I walk down to Charlotte's and eat supper with her and the children. Mac goes to his Ruritan Club that night and Joel goes off on his own until about nine when he picks me up. I see him coming up the walk and it's just like the old days when we were going out on a date — that's the feeling I get when I see him walking toward me. Like when he gets to where I am everything will be perfect. I love him that much, Livy, and want him every minute.

I hope you like your job better than at first. Well, what did you expect going off to Durham right by yourself to work with a lot of strangers in a tobacco factory? Didn't you know you'd be lonesome as all get-out? Why, I've been homesick myself. It's true. About a week after we got back from our honeymoon, right out of the blue I got this empty feeling in my chest so strong I almost cried. I wanted to go home so bad and here I am just a few miles from Charlotte's — I could walk if I had to. It was a physical pain, Livy, so I know what you've been going through.

I should tell you the good news, I guess, although I don't know what you'll think about it. Well, yes I do — but I'm telling you anyway! I'm going to have a baby! I missed in August but I didn't go see Dr. Frazier until September. Do you know how he tells? He feels! But it's not like Joel touching me, I promise you that. He (the doc) said he was almost certain I was pregnant and now my breasts are getting bigger and we're sure. I'm getting this poochy little belly, too, and I feel sickish in the mornings and sometimes I throw up. I haven't told anybody but Joel and now you. Joel didn't know what to think — I mean, he's happy and all but I don't think he believed it was going to happen so soon although he absolutely would not wear those rubber things and now it's too late.

He is doing fine — actually he doesn't love farming all that much and this summer was so hot and dry he nearly died from all the work but the tobacco was pretty and the market good so with me working we have enough to get by on. I suppose I will have to quit my job when I start looking fat. And I'm going to have to tell Charlotte soon. After all, she's got eyes and this past Thursday I thought she was staring at me funny but she never said a word. She is going to have a hissy-fit and we both know what that's like.

Well, it's almost time to start fixing supper which is going to be boiled cabbage and new sweet potatoes his daddy brought by. I don't know where Joel is. He's been gone all day in the truck when I was expecting him at noon. I intended to go to town and get a few things but we'll make do until Monday when I can shop during my lunch hour. Sundays we eat with his folks anyway.

Which reminds me, are you going to church up there? I am missing Shiloh more than I thought I would — I get to go now and then but Joel doesn't want to and his family eats at twelve o'clock sharp even if they don't have a thing to do all afternoon. Nobody visits them or anything. Sometimes Charlotte and Mac come by and take me out to Shiloh and then to Mama Bess's. I love that big old house! I tell Joel someday we'll have a place like that but he says first thing we have to do is provide for this little baby.

Oh, I hope you find somebody nice, Livy, and get settled down! Being married is the best thing in the world! Later I'll tell you what having a baby is like! I'm sure it's a girl and I've even named her Caroline in my mind. Do you like that? Caroline Calder. I think it's pretty enough to be in a book even if I thought of it myself.

Write back to me. I want to hear all the big city news. Do you remember how we used to read every book on Charlotte's shelf? I do. Have you read *Tender is the Night* by F. Scott Fitzgerald? She lent it to me this week and I've read a little. Do you know people like that, living in the city like you do? I just don't know them at all. I don't have much time for reading anyway — my nights are taken! Oh Livy, some of them are very tender —

ED

Course, I'd see him at work. Then of an evening, I'd stop by Hamm's and he'd be there, too, right regular it seemed like. I didn't stay long cause Annette was always expecting me. Looked like I spent about as much time with my girlfriend as he did with his wife. Course, that was just how it looked. They were together more than not. It was a different way of doing for both of them, I reckon. Always beholding to another. I can see where it would take some getting used to.

He'd get a couple of drinks in him and he'd be laughing and talking. Real friendly and having a good time. Nobody wanted to play poker for money by then, so the card games got right friendly, too. We were just a bunch of fellas, you know, trying to forget how bad things were and wondering how much worse they could get. We couldn't see much ahead of us, that's for damn sure.

BETHANY

About twilight I heated a pan of water on the stove and stripped to my slip in front of the kitchen sink to wash. I didn't even close the back door — nobody had reason to walk this way or could come by car without my hearing. I sponged off slowly while the rinse water hissed in the kettle. I let the water trickle over my arms and drip down to my elbows before I caught it again on the washcloth. Then I sent the cloth down between my breasts which were almost too tender to touch. Under my arms, across my shoulders. I loved the smell of the soap and the way the cooling water made my neck tingle and my arms raise gooseflesh.

He startled me. "Bethany, what are you doing?" he said through the screen. He said he'd knocked twice. "Where were you?" he wanted to know. I guess he could tell from watching me that I'd been somewhere else, off in a dream away from him.

Instead of answering, I dumped the soapy water down the drain and poured hot water in the pan.

"Bethany, the door's hooked," he said.

"I'm not finished with my bath yet," I said, still not looking at him. "You can't just come barging in while I'm bathing."

"What difference does it make?" he asked. "I'm standing right here looking at you, for God's sake. Why didn't you shut the door and close the curtains?"

"You don't have to bother with all that when you live at the end of the world," I said and dipped the tips of my fingers in the pan. The water was too hot so I fanned the surface with my hand. "All day I've been out here at the end of the world."

"Come on, Beth. Open the door." He leaned against the jamb now, casually, like he'd just wait till this little game was over. "You've got a starving man out here. What's for supper?"

"I ate a new potato and some boiled cabbage because that was all I had to fix. I don't know what you'll have. I'm eating for two, you know." The steam filled my throat with its misty warmth and I leaned over it, then filled my hands and brought the water to my face. It ran down my arms and dripped down my neck. I could feel my slip sticking to me.

"Let me in, Beth," Joel said, jerking at the hook. "Come on now. I'm getting tired of this."

I was standing in a little puddle of water.

"Bethany, I'm going to knock this goddamn door down!" He slapped the doorframe and the dishes in the breakfront rattled.

"And then what?" I turned to him without bothering to dry off.

"We'll go somewhere," Joel said. "We'll get dressed up and go to town, maybe even to Lawrence. What the hell, it's Saturday night! We'll find a party somewhere. There might even be a dance at a warehouse. We better get in some dancing before you're too big for me to hold on to. That's coming, you know, when you'll be too fat for anything." He pressed his weight against the doorframe, testing it. I knew he could push through but it would mean a broken screen to fix.

"Last year this time we were always together," I said. "You couldn't get enough of me then."

"I still can't," Joel crooned. "Open up, darling, and I'll show you."

"I'll have to heat the cabbage. Cold cabbage's not fit to eat."

"I don't mind. You know I'll eat anything." He grinned. I could see his teeth flashing, the outline of him pressed to the screen. It made him look gigantic, like he could take up my whole life.

Well, he did. He had. I went to the door and snapped up the hook, then backed away to let him through. I didn't open my arms. I didn't need to.

🌺 CHARLOTTE

I was in the kitchen working biscuit dough for supper when the front door slammed. I waited, my hands resting in the dough, to hear Patsy run down the hall or Davey's noisy creeping because he still loved to scare the living daylights out of you. Not a sound but steam spitting around the lid of the potatoes I was simmering. I wiped my hands and went down the hall, switching on lights as I went. No child in sight so I went on upstairs.

Bethany was lying on the bed in her old room. She'd dropped her shoes but still had her sweater on. Her feet and legs looked puffy and she had her arm over her face. I sat down on the edge of the bed.

"He'll be here soon," she said without looking at me. "When I'm not waiting, he'll come by here."

I knew she'd been standing in front of the bank at least an hour, until the traffic on the street disappeared and all the shops closed. Only the mill was open this late. "You can eat with us," I said. I wanted to rub her poor swollen feet but I didn't.

"No, he'll be along in a minute. I'll fix something at

home."

"He could eat here now and then, you know," I told her. "He used to often enough."

"We're not courting anymore." She moved her arm away from her face and uncurled her hand on the bedspread. I grasped her fingers and wrapped them in mine.

"I think I felt the baby move last night. Joel said he didn't feel a thing. He said it was in my head."

"Was it?"

"No, it's the baby growing right in here." She nodded down the length of her body, then put our palms on her belly. A warmth seemed to press up into our hands.

"I want you to be happy, Bethany," I said. "That's all I've ever wanted."

"I am," she said.

🌺 JOEL

It was after midnight when I got there. To Charlotte's, I mean. I knew that's where I'd find her after I went all the way out to the house and she wasn't there. Well shit, looks like she could just get a ride, but hell no, she has to walk to Charlotte's and let everybody know I'm a lazy no-good son of a bitch.

I could see somebody coming through the glass panels and I hoped it was Bethany, then we'd just sneak out and that'd be the end of it. But it was Charlotte looking at me through the pane. She had her hands pushed deep down in the pockets of her bathrobe and she was all bowed up. I didn't think she was going to let me in.

"Do you know what time it is?" she said. Through the glass, mind you.

Well, goddamn, I wasn't about to stand out there in the cold playing games with Charlotte Woodard. I wasn't going to act sorry, either. I'd just go back home and tomorrow tell Bethany how I tried to get her. I reckon Charlotte saw how it was because she unlocked the door right then.

"Where is she?" I asked in the hall.

"Where do you think? She's asleep." She was mad enough to spit nails. The sleeping house was the only reason she wasn't yelling. "Where have you been?"

"My business ran late," I said.

"Hah!" If looks could kill, she'd of had me then. "You've been drinking! Do you think I'm stupid?"

"No Ma'am. I don't give a good goddamn what you think." I went past her. I reckon I would of pushed her out of the way if she'd of tried to stop me but she didn't. I went up the stairs two at the time with her coming after me but I beat her to Bethany's door and shut myself inside before she reached me.

The room was so dark I had to wait a minute before I could see. When I could make her out, Bethany was turned toward me on the bed with her knees pulled up and her hands folded under her chin. I thought maybe the baby was sleeping like that too, curled up and kind of floating inside her.

Seeing her that way, I just about cried. I shouldn't of bet on that damn cock or stayed out there half the night trying to make up my losses. I should of done all what I promised — bundled the fodder, burned off that cornfield, picked her up by five like usual.

I dropped my jacket and pants on the floor, then pulled off my shirt and shoes and slipped into bed beside her. I worked myself around to her shape where I could breathe against her neck and feel her hair on my face. Her bottom was warm against me.

Oh, I'll love you, Beth. I'll take care of you. I promise I will.

That was what I thought.

❧ CHARLOTTE

The only blouse I had she could wear pulled a little bit across the bosom but she wore it anyway — that and her skirt from the day before. She ate a piece of dry toast and walked down to the bank while he slept upstairs. After she'd gone, I went out to sweep the front porch and there was his truck toed in toward the ditch like it had been driven too fast and abandoned. By noon everybody in town would know he and Bethany had stayed the night at my house; they'd surmise there was trouble between them. Of course, they'd already know she was pregnant if they bothered to look.

I couldn't stand to think about it. That's the truth. I couldn't bear to imagine her in labor when she ought to be going to college dances with boys headed for professional school. I swept right down the walk, flicking leaves off the broom into the grass while that old truck grinned at me, its grill curled up like a smirk.

That's when I turned around and marched right back up the walk, right upstairs. I didn't even knock. He was curled up like a baby with the spread tucked up under his chin. Even with a day-old stubble, he looked like a little boy. His hair was mashed against the pillow and his hand showed like he'd just pulled up the covers and left it there at his cheek.

I'd come to tell him to get up and get going, go do something to earn his keep and take care of that girl he'd ruined. Let's see you rise to your responsibility instead of going off drinking and gambling while Bethany stands on her poor swollen feet all day so you'll have something to eat of an evening.

But I didn't say it. The look of him stopped me. Why, he's a baby himself, I thought. Both of them are and what I've got to do is help them. I've got to put aside my own feelings.

I touched his shoulder. "Joel."

He lurched like he'd been struck. "What? What?"

"It's nine-thirty," I said. "I thought you might want to get going before long."

He was just figuring out where he was. "Where's Beth?"

"She's gone to work."

He rubbed his face hard. "Good God."

I stayed quiet.

"I didn't plan on being late." He pulled himself up in the bed but I don't think he knew what he was saying, or at least who he was saying it to.

"Well." I went to the door.

"I mean it, Charlotte."

"Bethany's the one who's got to know that, not me," I said before I stepped outside and shut the door. I could hardly get my breath and when I could, it hurt in my chest. I'd as soon take a whipping as be nice to him, but I was.

CHAPTER ELEVEN

🌿 BETHANY

I told Charlotte a fib. I stood right there in her kitchen while she and Milly made candy for the church shut-in boxes and told her I didn't want to go to Shiloh on Christmas Eve.

"Of course you do. It's a Malone tradition." Charlotte was cracking peanut brittle with a little hammer and the sugar crystals shattered around her hand. Patsy slipped between us to scoop up the slivers. "You know this isn't for us," Charlotte said but gave her a thick nutty piece anyway.

I popped a sliver in my mouth and waited for my tongue to prickle with its sweetness. "Maybe we want to start our own traditions."

"Huh." I could see Charlotte's shoulders tightening but she ignored me and went after Milly. "You just tested that fudge two minutes ago and it's as plain as day it's not ready," she said in that snippy tone of hers.

Milly dropped a narrow stream of syrup in a cup of water, anyway. "You ought to come, Bethany," she said. "All the children are in it. Why, Patsy here has the angel part. Say your lines for Bethany, honey, so she'll see how good you are. Wednesday at practice she said every word perfectly. Now listen, Bethany! Go on, Patsy! 'Fear not for, behold, I bring you good tidings. . .'"

Her voice trailed off but Patsy who was crunching on the sugary peanuts didn't take over.

"It's him, isn't it?" Charlotte said. "He doesn't want to come. He doesn't want to do a thing involving your family. I can see that."

I said, "It's not Joel." But of course it was.

Charlotte was layering the peanut brittle between waxed paper in a tin. "When Mac and I got married I told him, 'Look, there are many things that are negotiable, but holidays are not among them'."

"You said that to your husband?" Milly said. "Why, that sounds like a bank meeting!"

"A good marriage is a business," Charlotte said. "It's not all lovey-dovey like you still want to think, Milly."

"Don't talk to me!" Milly studied the spreading gob of chocolate in the water. "Wilton and I get along just fine without my bossing him around."

"I'm just saying that when something is very important to you, you have to let your feelings be known."

"It's not Joel," I told her. "It's not."

But that night, I missed them so! I missed the holly boughs in the window sills and the boxwood wreath on the door at Shiloh. I missed singing carols and seeing Patsy in the angel dress I wore years ago, even hearing Wilton's sermon — for three years he'd preached practically the same one about the shepherds, how they were poor, common folks just like ourselves and see what had happened to them, what could happen to US! I missed Mama Bess's kitchen full of women and the smell of cider and oyster stew and Aunt Lucille's Japanese fruitcake on the sideboard and little cups of homemade wine and a tree crowding the parlor.

I decorated a little white pine for us, put cranberries and popcorn on it, then a few chipped glass balls Charlotte had been putting on the back of her tree. Our front room was small but I hadn't had the time or the money to make it cozy yet, just an old sofa from the Calder house facing the fireplace. I curled up there on Christmas Eve, watching the fire in the dark and feeling pressed down with loneliness. It was like I was living in a foreign place. Huddled there, I felt a cold wind cross my shoulders.

It was Joel coming in with the coal bucket. He rubbed his hands together in front of the fire.

"How about a little drink for Christmas Eve? That'll warm us up." He was acting cheerful like this was the way Christmas ought to be.

"I'm warm," I said when the truth was I'd been shivering ever since we'd walked home from the Calder's an hour before. We'd eaten there but left early. Ed and Annette were going to a party somewhere.

"Come on and go with us," Ed had said but I couldn't squeeze into a decent dress anymore. I didn't feel like dancing anyway. So I helped Emma with the dishes and we came on home to the chilly house.

"Just a drop. A little Christmas spirit." Joel said and went to get the glasses.

I sipped at it but even a little put a fire in my throat and made my eyes water. "I can't believe you like this stuff."

He took a deep swallow. "I like how it makes me feel. That light feeling, you know, like my head's lit up inside. If you drink enough, you sort of spin out real slow and everything in your head just rests easy."

"That's called going unconscious," I said.

"Well, it feels mighty good." He sat down and wrapped his arm around me. "But not as good as you."

I let myself be held.

"They're opening presents about now," I said into his shoulder. "Then about midnight they'll sing 'Silent Night,' off-key of course, and go on home."

"I bet Ed and Annette are dancing their fool heads off," he said.

"You could have gone with them."

"Not without you."

"I'm too fat to breathe, much less dance."

"I think you're beautiful. I like my women plump."

"That's not so. You told me once that fat people make you sick."

He was nuzzling my neck. His breath was sweet with whiskey. "I told you lots of things back then."

"Was any of it true?"

"I reckon some of it was. Now what I remember best is how pretty you were that morning at the depot."

"You remember what you want to," I said.

Later I woke up clammy under the blankets but my face and shoulders were prickly with cold. Where his head rested against me there was the pounding ache like a cramped muscle. I wanted to move but his weight, and the baby's, locked me there. I could hear the ticking of the clock and Joel's wheezy breath. There wasn't a sound outside of us, no world beyond that room. I want to be happy here, I thought to myself. Please, God, let us be happy.

He moved then and the covers fell back with him. I lay there feeling the sharp cold moving down my body. I could get up if I wanted to. I could fly away into the night. Colored people could fly, Mena said. She said they could just lift right away from their troubles, that's how they survived so much suffering in this world.

"Beth?" I could feel his eyes in the dark, his searching fingers.

"Here," I said and put his hand against my heart. "Here I am."

🌸 CHARLOTTE

She left him sleeping, took the truck which couldn't have warmed up enough to stop her shivering, and came to my house. I was in the kitchen rolling out the cinnamon rolls so they could rise while we opened presents. That's what we've done for years — have coffee or hot cocoa, then after the presents we eat a big breakfast with cinnamon rolls the size of salad plates, scrambled eggs and yellow grits, thin cured ham that renders red-eye gravy full of salt and spice to pool in the grits.

"You came," I said when the kitchen door opened and there she was, alert with cold, her little belly straining the buttons of her winter coat. "I thought about you all last night."

"I wanted to see the tree," she said. "I wanted —"

I made her stop. My arms hushed her and we hugged for a moment before she pulled away. "Let's look then," I said.

In the parlor, she dropped her coat on a chair and plugged in the tree lights. It burst into color, the ornaments catching light on every curve.

"It's beautiful, isn't it? Mac and Davey spent the whole morning looking for it. They went all the way to Lawrence because I wanted a fir. Doesn't it smell wonderful?"

"It's beautiful," she said.

I knew she had noticed the stockings — three of them — bulging full above the firelight.

"We fixed your stocking like always. Mac said if you didn't come today, we'd take it out to you. A girl in the family way still wants a Christmas stocking, doesn't she?"

"Yes." She turned her face away.

"Well, come help me fix the oranges for breakfast," I said. "The children will be down here any minute."

We drank coffee while we halved and sectioned the oranges. Then there were squeals from the parlor. "I should go," Bethany said. "I left Joel a note in case he woke up but I didn't come to stay. I just wanted to wish you a merry Christmas."

"But you have to be here when we open our presents," I said. "And for breakfast. Eat breakfast with us."

"Now that it's winter, some days he sleeps all morning," she said, looking out the window at the cold yard, the gray shed rimmed with frost.

"Then stay," I begged her. And she did.

🌸 MAC

About noon, we heard the screen door slap the wall like it was being thrown off it hinges. Next, hard pounding that could splinter wood.

"I'll go," I said because I saw Bethany's face. She was frowning at the mantel clock which was about to strike noon. Charlotte started to collect wrapping paper. Her hands went white when she crushed it into fierce little balls. We all knew who it was.

He pushed into the hall the second I released the latch, before I could say anything to stop him. Then she was coming, too. She rushed past Charlotte who put out her hands to catch her but couldn't. The clock was striking. Paper rustled around the children's feet as they followed from the parlor.

"Oh, I'm so glad you came!" Bethany said to him. "We've been having the best time! Come see what Santa brought Davey and Patsy. And me, too, Joel! Santa filled my stocking just like always! Come see!"

But he didn't move. His mouth was stiff with cold and the hair around his cap looked brittle. He slapped his hands against his thighs, the knuckles swollen and red. Cold from the open door swept around us but nobody moved.

"Oh, you walked and now you're frozen! Come in and get warm. Charlotte, is there coffee left? Or cocoa? That would be good, wouldn't it?"

His arm went up. We all saw it, saw how she didn't back

away but seemed to sink into the raw hand that caught her jaw like something hurled hard and frozen through the air.

"No!" Charlotte screamed. "Don't!" But it was too late. The slap sang across her cheek, then bounced up the bridge of her nose. Patsy was screaming. She and Charlotte filled the house with shrieks. Bethany didn't make a sound. I tried to take hold of her but she wouldn't let me. She moved forward, her red streaked face held high to him who by then had tears in his own eyes and snot collecting at the rim of his nose. He put his arms out and she was there before I could stop her.

"Oh God," he moaned. They seemed to crumple against each other. She flung his cap away and put her hands in his stiff curls, her fingers wrapped over his ears. She arched her back to take on his weight and held him close like she would comfort him.

"It's all right," she whispered in his hair. "It's all right." Over and over again she said it.

I said, "Charlotte, get some coffee."

She didn't budge. "I want him out of this house."

"Wait a minute," I said. "Let's let them handle this."

"He hit her!"

I put my arm around Patsy and, with my free hand, herded Davey back into the parlor. "See about the coffee, Charlotte," I said.

But while she was in the kitchen and I had the children in the parlor, we heard the truck rev up. Charlotte came running but it was too late.

"She didn't take her presents!" She was frantic.

"She'll be all right," I said.

"No, she won't. He'll hit her again if he's a mind to."

"Something just came over him, Charlotte. He didn't know what he was doing."

"And you defend him!" She grabbed Patsy out of my grip and held her smothering tight. "If anybody ever tries to hit you, honey, you come to me!" she said. "Don't you stand there and take it!"

"Is Bethany going to have a big dinner like we are?" Patsy was wet-faced and sniffling.

"Yes sir-ree bob. I bet she's getting it ready right now," I said.

"Huh! They probably don't have a thing in the house. If she weren't working they'd be worse off than any sharecropper I know of. And what's going to happen when the baby comes? She can't work then!" Charlotte's mouth was a quivery line. "Oh, I've got to do something! But what? What can I do?"

"We'll figure something out," I told her.

BETHANY

During the night a snow fell, so in the morning our bedroom was as bright as midday. It was more than a foot deep, Joel said when he brought in the little bit of coal we had left.

I stayed in bed while he went ahead and got the cookstove going. We had a little store of firewood. My cheek hurt. Once during the night, I woke with a start — maybe it was the stillness of the snowfall that startled me — and when I turned my head, there was a pop in my jaw and a hot spike of pain. I lay still for a long time waiting for it to go away but it never did.

I was hungry, too. Since breakfast at Charlotte's, all I'd had was a glass of buttermilk and some leftover beans that tasted half spoiled. The Calders were expecting us but how could I go like I looked, so Joel went over there and made some excuse, didn't even wait for his mother to fix us plates which she would have done. He came home in the sleet, all wet and cold and looking like I should feel bad for him. Not once did he say he was sorry.

"Beth?" He was bringing me coffee. The odor reached me before he did. It was thick and vile, not like coffee at all, and I rolled away from him, over the edge of the bed, and raked my hands on the floor searching for the slopjar before the heaving started.

"Holy shit," he said. "I thought that was all over with."

"It's the coffee," I said between retches and he backed away, taking the cup with him. The rest of the day he didn't say a word.

❧ MAC

That snow just about closed down the county. There came a hard freeze after it so for several days nothing much moved. I couldn't get the car out so I walked to the mill just to keep up with the paperwork. Heber Bronson opened his grocery store and Doug Watson got himself to the bank but the tellers didn't come. The town looked like it was sleeping, taking a rest after the hub-bub of Christmas.

The first day I could, I went out there to see Joel. He was in the yard trying to get the truck started. It was cold and the wind was huffing but the sun was out. They had icicles a foot long dripping along the porch roof but there was a little trickle of smoke coming out the chimney.

"I didn't know how the road was, so I brought a few supplies," I told him. Charlotte had packed up milk and butter, a bag of dried fruit, a piece of ham and some canned goods along with the little gifts from Bethany's Christmas stocking. I put them on the porch when he didn't offer for me to go in.

"Bethany doing all right?" I asked him.

"Sleeping," he said. "She's like a little old mama bear hibernating." He kept on tinkering under the hood.

"Road's passable now. Doug Watson says the bank'll be opened regular tomorrow."

"I'll tell her." His hands came out of the belly of the truck. They were streaked with axle grease.

"What happened the other morning," I said. "We've been mighty worried about it."

"Needn't be." He wiped his hands on a rag and got in the

cab. The truck started up, chugging at first and then idling fine. He cut the engine and got out.

"Things go better when a man treats a woman gentle," I said.

"We're doing all right." He dropped the hood and it clanged like ice breaking in the quiet. "You tell Charlotte. You tell her everything's just fine out here."

🌸 BETHANY

All day at the bank, I talked to Joel in my head. Sometimes to the baby. Sometimes to Charlotte but that was always an argument. Charlotte never came to the bank — Mac was who I saw. Joel was picking me up every night then. He'd take me home, then most nights he'd go out again. I don't know where he got the money.

The kitchen was the only warm room in the house so I'd prop my feet in a straight chair and sleep sitting up an hour or more, till I'd wake up stiff and with a crick in my neck. Sometimes it was the quiet that woke me up startled and I'd think, "He's dead. He's in a ditch between here and Hamm's." But he always came home eventually. It was wintertime and he was bored with not much to do on the farm. That made him restless and out of sorts so he needed some fun. I thought in the spring everything would be different. He'd have work and I'd be warm again. We'd have our baby.

Mac gave me money for Dr. Frazier. He offered to pay for the hospital, too, but I wanted to have the baby at home. Dr. Frazier said that was all right with him. I wanted Mena with me. Charlotte, too, but I didn't ask her. She'd suit herself, anyway.

February turned bitter again and the low place in the road was covered with ice every day. Once Joel skidded taking the curve too quick and slung me against the door so hard a bruise came on my temple and the next morning my neck was stiff so I had to stand at an angle in my cubicle. Milly came in that day with her baby Sarah bundled in her arms. Her sweet cherub face was rosy with cold. After they'd gone, I pressed my hands under my belly, pushing my baby as tight as I could into the protection of my ribcage. All of a sudden, it seemed too exposed. Even the maternity clothes Milly lent me were tight and my coat didn't cover anymore.

I didn't sleep much by then either. I couldn't turn without waking. Joel didn't sleep curled against me anymore and I know I seemed impossible to him. He said I felt hard everywhere.

"Well, so do you," I said and put my hand on him under the covers. He swelled up every time I touched him but that wasn't often. Most nights I was too tired or it was too late or he smelled of whiskey. I could hardly remember how it used to be, how he was hot all over me so I'd lose my breath from it. More than once that summer we'd made love before we could even get to the bedroom; one time with my legs wrapped around the rungs of a straight chair he was sitting in, once on the backporch before it was even dark good.

"You're so different now," he said one Saturday afternoon when it was too cold to walk anywhere and the truck was on empty. I was washing Mama's china although it wasn't dusty. It was something to do.

"I am not," I told him. "And if I am, so are you."

"I don't want us to be different," he said.

I lifted one of Mama's plates out of the dishwater. Wet like that, it glistened like it was really fine.

"Put that down," he said. "Let's do something."

"There's nothing to do." I put the plate on the drainboard.

"Let's play cards."

"After I finish this," I said because there were two more plates in the suds.

"No, now."

"The water'll get cold if I don't finish," I said.

"I don't give a damn."

Before I could stop him, he was reaching around me to the

drainboard.

"Don't," I screamed at him. "That's all I've got of Mama's!" But the plate was leaving his hand. I saw it quivering in the air before it hit the wall. Pink roses scattered on the floor.

"Now will you stop?" he yelled. "Will you just stop?"

"You bastard!"

"You don't give a damn about me! You never did!" He tried to take my shoulders. I knew he wanted me to deny it but I didn't. Instead I wrenched away and bent down to pick up the plate. The ragged edge caught on my thumb.

"You're bleeding." I could see he was scared. "Bethany, you're bleeding."

For a minute he was the person I used to know but I didn't care. I held my hand away from him.

🌺 JOEL

I know I didn't do right. Nobody has to tell me that. It got to where lots of nights I'd take her home and just go on out again. Sometimes I didn't even turn off the truck, just set there with it running while she went on in the house. More than likely I'd go to Lawrence and find a card game or get to playing pool and lose track of time. Sometimes she'd be in bed when I got back. I could see where she'd left her clothes on a kitchen chair — she got undressed by the stove. Sometimes there'd be something cold for me to eat, sometimes not.

One night I boxed. She'd left me supper but I couldn't eat, not with a busted lip, so I left it on the table and went on to bed. I knew she wasn't asleep. I could feel her eyes on me the minute I went in the bedroom. I dropped my pants on the floor and crawled in beside her. The sheets were slick with cold and I lay quiet, trying to make myself a warm spot.

"Are you hurt?" I reckon she could smell blood on me.

"They had boxing at Planters Warehouse and I lost a

tooth. I've been spitting blood all the way home."

She found my cheek with her hand. I felt her fingers traveling across my swollen mouth. My lip was sore at the split. "Are you really all right?"

"Yeah."

"What if something happened to you? What would I do?" She rested her head on my chest. Her hair was across my neck, warming me there.

"You'd be all right," I told her.

"Did you win the fight?"

"Yeah. Ten dollars."

"You lost a tooth for ten dollars?"

"It doesn't show." I moved my fingers in her hair. The tangles felt like webs. "You can get the baby something with the money."

"Charlotte's giving me what she saved of Patsy's baby clothes. Milly has some, too. It'll be fine."

"I want you really bad," I said.

"I can tell."

"I probably taste terrible."

She touched my torn lip. I hugged her as close as I could with the baby between us.

"So you went to make some money for the baby," she whispered.

"No." I was holding her tight. "I just wanted to beat the hell out of somebody."

CHAPTER TWELVE

🌺 CHARLOTTE

The baby shower Milly was planning wouldn't be a surprise without Joel's help so I went out there one morning to talk to him about it. He was over at J.C.'s mending a mule harness. While I talked, he ran his fingers up and down the leather like he was touching fur or maybe a string of pearls. His knuckles were torn and his hand already tanned and rough from spring planting but it was graceful on the leather and I watched without meaning to.

"Well, Milly's good to be planning a little get-together." He popped the leather hard against his thigh.

I winced but went on explaining. "We could make it a surprise if she came to eat with us like she used to. That way I could get her to walk down to Milly's on some pretense."

He lay the harness over the fence and pushed his hat back but he didn't say anything. He was making me wait on purpose. I wanted to slap him so bad my arm ached but I just stood there in the hot sun looking at him. He was too good-looking for words, that's true. Even in dusty workclothes, with a few days stubble on his jaw and chin, he was handsome. More handsome even than on his wedding day when he'd been wearing a suit J.C. must have paid dearly for. They were going to have the prettiest baby in the world.

"I don't see why I can't manage it. I'll tell Beth I've got to be in Lawrence all afternoon. On business." He was grinning.

I wanted to ask him what kind of business he had that wasn't tended to in some dark alley or backroom somewhere but I held my tongue. I could feel an ache crawling across my shoulders and up my neck. "Well then," I said. "You come by Milly's about nine to get her. Either that or she can spend the night with us."

"I'll be there," he said. He straightened his hat brim over his eyes and picked up the harness again. I was dismissed.

The fumes in the car made me nauseous and I drove too fast going back to town. I just wanted to get home.

By the time I got there, my head was splitting. Mena was out there shaking the dust mop over the side of the front porch, never mind that I'd told her a thousand times to do it in the back, but my head hurt so bad I couldn't even reprimand her. I leaned into the car door, trying to push it open. She saw and came to get me. Practically dragged me in the house.

"You been out there makin yourself sick." Her voice pushed through the curl of pain in my temple.

I collapsed on the sofa. "I just wish she'd go ahead and have that baby, just get it all over with." Nerves behind my eyes grabbed and squeezed.

Mena slipped a powder off the paper into my mouth and held the water for me to drink. Then she put the cloth across my face and pressed it to my eyes and temples. "You goes and does till this happens," she said.

The cloth made a thin darkness over my eyes and soothed me a little. I reached out for Mena's hand. Her grip was dry and strong. "If anybody comes, don't you let on I'm sick like this."

At the baby shower, Hazel Watson told me all about how well Douglas was doing in school at Chapel Hill. She and Doug were hoping he'd want to come home afterwards and work at the bank. Eventually take over, she meant, and be important in the town. Patsy, Lizzie and Olivia were there, giggling and rattling their dishes on their knees like juveniles. Well, they were children still. Bethany, too, although she was so poked out by then she couldn't rest her plate on her lap. I couldn't look at her without feeling sick so I concentrated on Milly's refreshments. She'd fixed pink punch and salted pecans and decorated the cake with little pink paper umbrellas. She'd even found napkins with fat pink babies on them. It was very nice.

❧ BETHANY

Putting the baby gifts in the dresser, I put my hand on a revolver. It was like the one Mac kept in his desk drawer at the mill. He'd offered to bring it home one time when Charlotte was beside herself about derelicts drifting south but she'd been furious over the idea. "Do you think I'd have a weapon in this house with these children?" she wanted to know. She might as well have called him a fool to his face the way she said it.

The gun in the dresser was short-nosed and ugly. I turned out the chamber and saw it was loaded, then I put it back in the drawer and sat down on the bed, the baby clothes still clutched to my chest. Why was it there, hidden like that? It's for protection, I decided — why else would it be loaded? I'd just ask him about it.

"Beth!"

I jumped up facing the dresser mirror and saw I looked wild, like I was scared without even knowing it. I lay the clothes on the dresser and turned to him.

"What is it?" he asked. He was tracking fertilizer across the floor and its hot smelly dust bounced in the air around him.

"Nothing." My heart was fluttering in my throat.

"You sure? You're not having pains, are you?"

"No. Dr. Frazier says I can go another week, maybe two. I'm fine."

"Well in that case, I hope supper's ready. I'm starving." He was in a good mood.

"First you need a bath," I said.

"No, afterwards. I'm empty as a drum. I'll eat on the porch. It's warm enough."

We ate on the backsteps while pans of water heated on the stove for his bath. Then I brought the soap and a towel while he filled the washtub with water. He stripped out of his old canvas pants and dusty shirt.

I started back into the kitchen to do the dishes but he said "Stay," so I waited. It had been all winter since I'd seen him naked in stark daylight. His body was tanned in places like farmboys always are and the pale skin of his chest and shoulders were doused with light freckles. The slight curving valleys where his shoulders met his breastbone looked especially pale and soft, eager to be touched. His body hair was fine and golden.

"You, too," he said with laughing in his voice.

"What?" but I knew his meaning. "No," I said and felt a blush down my throat.

"Nobody'll see," he said.

"You will." I started unbuttoning my blouse. "I'm a sight."

"I know it." He stepped into the tub.

There was hardly room for both of us so I lay against his chest with his arms wrapped around me. The sky was turning mauve beyond the white field. The scent of fertilizer was strong in the air but we smelled only the soap, our damp hair and sweaty skin in the sweet water. His hands were on my belly, lingering on my swollen breasts. His lips nibbling on my neck sent shivers everywhere.

Oh, this is what matters, I thought as we lay together in water as comforting as a womb. Just this.

🌺 JOEL

I thought she'd peed in the bed but when I turned on the light, we were lying in a puddle of bloody water.

"It's the baby," she said. "The baby's coming."

"But the doc said it's not time. Maybe something's wrong," I said.

"No, it's all right." She looked pale, though. "I've got to have this baby some time, don't I?"

"I'll go get the doctor." I was hunting in a dark corner for my pants.

"No, don't. I haven't had a real contraction yet. You can wait till daylight. I'll tell you when."

"I think I ought to go now," I told her.

"Just bring some towels to put over this mess and come back to bed. This might be the last night we'll be alone until we're old and gray."

So I did. I lay down again with my hand against her belly and her head on my shoulder. When I woke up again, the sun was edging the horizon and she was holding back a cry.

All We Know of Heaven

CHAPTER THIRTEEN

🌸 MENA

First thing he done, he woke up his daddy so it's Mr. J.C. come to town and gets me. Going on seven, I knocks at the Woodard's. Mr. Mac come down, nothin but his pants on. Miss Charlotte come after him. Hair loose, barefoot. She got on a raggedy old summer gown ought to be in the ragbag. I put it there, too, first chance I got. I tells them what Mr. J.C. says, how it's comin fast and fierce and she starts in yellin.

"Oh God, he's waited too long! Tell Bethany I'm coming!" She go flyin up them stairs like a haint's after her.

I goes ahead with Mr. J.C. and starts what needs doing — sweep up the kitchen floor and gets water a-boilin while Joel looks for a 'ceiving blanket, some heavy twine and them boiled scissors Bethany done wrapped up in a clean towel. Found it in the bottom drawer of the sideboard in a Christmas box. Bout then Miss Charlotte come cryin at us, "Where is she? Where's my chile?"

"The doctor's with her," Joel says right calm, never mind how she's carryin on.

"I's makin coffee," I tells her. "I can make up some biscuits, too, if folks is hungry."

"We didn't come here to eat," she says to me.

"Go ahead and make them," Joel says.

Miss Charlotte takes herself out on the back porch to wait for the doctor. She out there pacin and fidgetin. When Doc come in the kitchen, she all but tore the screen off gettin to him first.

He says how she comin long fine but it's still goin be awhile. Most the day, he says.

"I'm going in there with her," Miss Charlotte says. "I came prepared to stay."

Doc say he can come again bout noon.

"But that's four hours," Joel says. "She can't stand four hours of this."

"Yes, she can," Miss Charlotte says to him. "It's you who can't take it."

Doc set down there at the table and drank hisself a cup of coffee and ate two biscuits with Miz Bess' pear preserves on them. He said he never ate so light a biscuit in all his days. More than likely the truth, too. I knows how to make a biscuit.

🌹 JOEL

I couldn't stand the look on her face. She'd go ugly and twisted every time a pain struck. Between times, I'd touch the cool cloth Charlotte kept putting on her forehead. You could feel it gathering heat like she had a fever but she didn't. Once I tried to hold her hand while she was hurting but her fingers fought against me. She grabbed the neck of her gown like she was choking. It was like anything that touched her hurt. Nothing I could do helped her.

At noon, Mama came down with some dinner. Stewed corn and a pork roast that smelled mossy and rich. I couldn't eat but Doc Frazier was back by then and he had himself a plate at the kitchen table. Charlotte didn't eat either. She wouldn't come out of the bedroom except to pee. I was leaning against the truck smoking when she passed on her way to the outhouse and she acted like I wasn't there.

By two in the afternoon, I could hear Bethany all the way out in the yard. Between yells, I could still hear her. It was like the sound got trapped in the air so it couldn't move. My stomach gnawed but I didn't try to eat. Now and then I peeped in the bedroom. Charlotte was sitting on the bed, there where my baby had been made, where it was being born. I didn't go in.

"It ain't bad as it sound," Mena said to me in the yard. "Some women needs to holler, some be right quiet. You can't go by it."

"She could die," I said. "I know that."

"She doin fine," Mena said.

"I ought to be in there." I reckon she could see I was getting the jitters.

"Law, Mr. Joel, that ain't no place for a man. You can see her all you wants in a little while."

About three Bethany called my name on a long, high scream. Then Charlotte yelled, too. "Go get Fred," she said and I went, grinding the gears on the truck and slinging around corners till I pulled up at his office. Took me less than five minutes. Left the motor running while I raced inside, went right past folks in the waiting room and the nurse in the hall. "Now!" I yelled at him in the little examining room where a old man Connor had his shirt off. "Charlotte says right now!"

I followed Doc back out to the house. Rode in his dust so thick it blinded me. When we got there it was all quiet and he went on in the bedroom and shut the door. I stood there panting against the wall. I was lightheaded from too many smokes and the sun on the windshield.

"Something's wrong," I said to Mena when she came out looking grim. She was tying her headrag in a tight little knot.

"What foolishness is you talkin? That girl havin a baby is all. I ain't sayin it don't hurt some."

Then there was a grunting noise, low like a growl. Like the ground was pushing open.

"That done it," Mena said to me. "Sure as the world, that done it."

We heard a high wail.

"See there!" Mena was grinning. She swayed and swung her arms like she was going to dance. "Now we be needin that water I got coolin. We got ourselves a baby to wash."

When they let me in, Bethany looked unconscious. The baby was in her arms, wrapped up tight. Just a tiny dark smashed face showed out of a hole in the blanket. That was all right. I could look at her later. It was Bethany I needed to see. I put my hand over hers and she opened her eyes.

"Oh." She seemed too tired to talk.

"You did it." I brushed my lips against her cheek. She felt cool now.

She shut her eyes.

"Is she all right?" I asked Charlotte who was hovering around messing with the cradle.

"She will be."

"And the baby?"

"She's small. Fred says she could be as much as two weeks early and those last days are when a baby gets its weight."

She put her hand on my arm. No grip. Just resting there a second or two.

"She's going to sleep awhile now so you might as well go do something. Take Mena home. Go by and tell Mac I'm staying the night out here. Your folks will be wanting the news, too. I imagine they're on pins and needles over there."

It was the most she'd ever said to me at one time. "I'll do that." I put my hand on Bethany's cheek. "You tell her I'll be back soon."

Coming back from town, I stopped at home and waited on the back steps for somebody to find me. Somehow I couldn't make myself just bust in with the news. Daddy came out of the barn in a little bit and sat down on the step beside me.

"It's a girl," I told him. "I haven't got a real good look at her yet, but they say she's fine."

"And Bethany?"

"She's worn out but I reckon she'll be as good as new." The sky was deepening over the barn. It was going on six o'clock.

Daddy slapped me lightly on the back, then squeezed on a tight muscle he found there. I leaned sideways a little, almost resting under his arm.

"You all right, boy?"

"Yessir. I was worried, though. She's everything to me."

"Yeah, well. A woman sure can do that to you."

"I want to do right." Just saying it made me start tearing up. Daddy kept his arm around me.

"What is it?" Mama asked from the doorway. I could see how she'd been expecting the worst.

"Joel's got himself a baby girl," Daddy said. His voice was choked up bad as mine. "Now ain't that fine?"

"I reckon it is," she said.

🍀 BETHANY

I can't say what it was like for him, but I know this much: our house was full of people. He'd come home from work at noon and Charlotte would be there. Patsy, too, hanging on the cradle. Sometimes Mama Bess. We'd be talking about constipation, enflamed breasts, sitz baths. It would have embarrassed him if he'd been paying attention but he wasn't.

Sometimes Milly would be there sitting at the kitchen table drinking a glass of tea with me while her little one napped on our bed. Milly had more advice about babies than any book could have. Old school friends came, too, and friends of Charlotte's and Mama's who had always known the Malone girls and now knew me because I had a baby. It made me one of the tribe, I guess, more than just getting married could. Being married involves another person in a way you can't talk about but having a baby is a thing you do yourself. You can tell about it.

Joel would fix his own dinner. Most days it was meat stuffed between light bread or crumbly biscuits, a cold sweet potato he'd eat like fruit and a glass of sweet milk. He'd eat on the back porch. If Charlotte brought a pie or some cake, he'd eat that, too.

Pretty soon, the baby got colicky. It would strike at six in the afternoon and last till just about nine so our evenings were taken with screaming. I'd walk around the kitchen table or back and forth in the yard while she held her little body stiff and turned red and breathless with yelling. I'd cry with her.

Sometimes Joel would take her. "Poor Caroline," he'd croon, leaning over the scrunched-up face. She would curve her tiny mouth downward into her quivering little chin and suck in air for another wail while he talked to her. His two hands could support her head to toe.

I remember one time while he was holding her, her little mouth softened right up and her hands quit jerking like something had gotten her attention. He was crooning and nestling her and she went right on to sleep.

When I told Charlotte about it, she said, "Well, she must have passed enough gas to get comfortable." I know he soothed her, though.

JOEL

Bethany told Mr. Watson she'd be back to work by late June. I didn't like it a damn bit but what could I do? No yield on the crops till fall and we needed the money. I got to thinking maybe I should of gone to Baltimore a long time ago. By now I'd have a real job, not just sharecropping for my daddy. I might as well of been black as the ace of spades, working like I was. But I couldn't leave Bethany, not since that morning at the depot I couldn't. It all came down to her.

Charlotte figured out about taking the baby to work. She'd

put her expensive baby carriage down in the bank for Caroline to sleep in. At noon, Bethany would push the carriage down to Charlotte's and eat dinner. Then Charlotte could keep her awhile before wheeling her back to the bank. Most afternoons, Charlotte went down to the drug store about three anyhow, to have a fountain Coca-Cola and a package of nabs. The place would be packed with women of a summer afternoon, like a party.

"It'll work out fine," Bethany said to me but I didn't want to hear about it. I got right up from the supper table, left a half-full plate and went out for a smoke.

After awhile she came out and slipped her arms around me from behind. She put her cheek on my shoulder and just rested there.

"We both know it can't stay like this," she said. "Besides, I like the bank. I like seeing people and hearing what's going on around town."

So that was it. She wanted a life bigger than me and our baby.

🌺 BETHANY

He'd bring her to me in the night. He'd change her, too, while her little body kicked and squirmed, mouth rooting the air.

"It's coming, it's coming," I'd hear him sing while he bundled her up again. "All right, sweet little girl, all right."

In his arms, she'd be quiet and then I'd feel them near, his bending to lay her on my chest. Already my nipples would be wet, like they could hear her hungry, sucking noise. She hardly ever cried anymore. At two months when the colic was over, so was her crying.

I'd pull myself up against the headboard and open my gown to her. Sometimes, he'd slip behind me, making a pillow of himself for me to rest on. That way he held us both and if we fell asleep, he'd stay there the rest of the night with his head nodding against mine. He loved us.

🌹 WARREN

They thought I was a old hound dog, always sniffing around, but the truth is I saw it in the paper. Charlotte put it in there sure as the world just like she put that picture when they got married but it was too late that time. I wouldn't of come anyhow, not wanting to cause a ruckus.

What I mean is, I knew she was married and what her name was so when I saw about Mr. and Mrs. Joel Calder having a little baby girl, I knew it was her. I thought, well, I ain't going do nothing about it, and for awhile I let it lie. But then I got to thinking how that youngun was my flesh and blood and I ought to have myself a little look-see.

First off, I got a ride to Whitney. Then I went to the mill and asked Mac Woodard where I'd find her. He told me but didn't offer nothing else. I walked out there so I was pretty near winded when I knocked at the door and she come, holding that precious little thing in her arms. Pretty baby. Reminded me of Bethany herself.

She let me in and set me down at the table with a glass of tea and a piece of egg custard pie. She could see I was wore out. Anybody could. I'd been sick awhile.

"I was just about to change her," Bethany said and left me there in the kitchen. That's when he come in. Stopped dead in his tracks inside the kitchen door like he was looking on a terrible sight. Well, I reckon he was.

"I take it you're Joel," I said, cordial-like.

"And who the hell are you?" he says.

Bethany comes back with the baby about then. "Why, it's Daddy," she says, so sweet. "It's taken him all day to get here."

That boy just stood there. I could see he wasn't about to put his hand out so I reached for the baby and bless her heart,

Bethany handed her to me. I was weak and trembly but I held her steady. Bethany kneeled down on the floor beside me ready, I reckon, to grab hold if need be.

"She looks just like you did," I says. "Well, just about." I can tell you, I was ready to blubber. I looked at her husband. He was standing there all clenched up like he wanted to take a swing. "There's a smattering of you, too, here about the chin," I said to him. "Plain as day." The little thing was getting wiggly and about ready to tune up.

"Here, let me have her," Bethany said and I give her back. It was a relief, you know, because she was getting heavy on my arm.

Bethany sat down with her in the rocking chair there in the kitchen. I watched her lift her blouse and draw the baby's head to her bosom. She closed her eyes a minute, getting settled.

"Ah well, that's a beautiful sight, now ain't it?" I says to him but he's out the door. I heard the truck start up meaning I'd have to walk all the way back to town. Never mind. Sitting there, seeing the two of them that way, it was worth the miles.

CHAPTER FOURTEEN

🌹 CHARLOTTE

George and Lucille's boy Trax was getting married to a girl over in Lenoir County so naturally we were all invited. The invitations came in the mail, heavy cream-colored engraved ones. Extravagant like her people had money to burn.

"Maybe they've been saving for it all her life," Bethany said. She had just put the baby down and she stirred a little in her cradle.

"By now most folks are eating their savings." The Broydan's box I'd brought was on the bed. "Open it," I said.

When she lifted the pink silk dress and swung it free of the paper, I watched her face change just like that. Bright, then dark in a moment's time. "You shouldn't have," she said but held it up to herself anyway. It transformed her, face and all.

"You wouldn't believe the time I had finding something pretty like this that buttons down the front so nursing's not a problem and yet has something happening at the waist," I said. "It's the perfect dress for you to wear to Trax's wedding."

"Charlotte, I never said I was going." She was seeing herself in the mirror.

"Well, I RSVP'd for all of us. Just try it on. You're going to feel wonderful in it, like you used to —" I thought she'd bolt but she didn't. I went on, "It's important we look our best. After all, Trax is family and these are people we don't know."

She was just standing there with the dress against her bosom, looking fractious and undecided.

"Just try it. I didn't go all the way to Lawrence without expecting to at least see you in it."

She handed it to me and slipped out of the old school dress she was wearing. There were dark round stains on her brassiere where her milk had leaked.

"Make sure your titties are covered good," I told her. "We don't want to get anything on it." Her breasts were so full the flesh peeked out under her arms and her tummy pooched in front, as round and solid as a ball, but I could see how her waist was beginning to nip in a little.

"Did I ever tell you what Mama's oldest sister Geneva used to say about bosoms? Poor thing, she was a flat-chested woman in a family that mostly came well-endowed. Well, she used to tell us girls, 'What God has forgotten, we fill in with cotton.' She did it, too. Her dress front was always lumpy looking."

The dress slid over Bethany's head, then slipped down her body as soft as a cloud. Looking at her just about brought tears to my eyes.

"Oh, honey, you're beautiful in it," I said.

🌸 BETHANY

"I told Charlotte we'd go." I was pointing at the splattered invitation Joel had been ignoring for weeks. "Mac and Charlotte are leaving Saturday morning and coming home Sunday after the wedding. There'll be a reception, of course, so it'll be late but —"

"No," he said.

But I wouldn't let him stop me like that. "Uncle George is

taking Mama Bess and Papa Rowe and, of course, Harry and Lizzie'll be there. She's a bridesmaid. Milly and Wilton would go, too, but he has to preach at Shiloh. Milly is so disappointed but I told her I'm sure there'll be pictures to look at later on."

"I'm not going and neither are you." He was looking at me from under that shock of rusty curls because he still hadn't had a summer haircut. He looked like a little boy with his mouth set like that but I went on with what I'd planned.

"Well, I understand your not caring a thing about it, although you and Trax are friends, aren't you? Anyway, some people just don't like social functions and that's all right. It's fine. But I want to go. Trax has always been good to me. When I first came to live at Charlotte's, I was so lonesome and the cousins helped, they truly did."

He didn't budge. "It's one night," I said to him. "I suppose you've forgotten all the nights I've spent out here alone — well, until one or two in the morning at least, sleeping in this very chair or awake and worrying that you were dead somewhere." I got up and took my plate to the sink. "It's just a wedding, Joel. It's family."

"Hell, I know what it is!" I heard his hand coming across the table behind his voice, the swoosh of his arm before he flung dishes everywhere. The vinegar cruet went flying, splashing on the floor, skinny green peppers scattering. A bowl of butter beans cracked against the stove, sizzling juice on the hot iron. Pork chop bones sailed like thrown blades.

"Stop it," I screamed, too mad to back off. I flung my weight on him, pushing him down in his chair. I wrapped my arms around him and forced his head against my breasts. My fingers laced through his hair, holding him. He could have pushed me away, I know that, but he didn't. I could feel my heart pounding. "Don't do this," I said in his ear, determined to hold on until I felt him relax against me. He moaned a little and his breath caught in his chest.

"I don't know what gets into me." He was leaning into me hard.

"It's all right, darling." I ran my fingers into the neck of his shirt and kneaded a knotted muscle there. "You're all right. Sh-h-h."

It seemed like I held him a long time. The scorched beans gave off a smoky stench. The dish water steamed and hissed in the kettle. My arms and breasts ached. From where I was, I could see the room, the havoc he'd made. It seemed like my whole life was strewn there and all I held was emptiness.

JOEL

She went. She handed Caroline to Charlotte, then climbed in the car herself and settled by the window, took Caroline back and held her up to me, flapping her little arm like she was old enough to wave. I waved back and went on in the house.

There was a lot needed doing around the place. I could see that. I could fix the back door hinge. Bring a load of wood closer to the porch, maybe tighten the clothesline post. Make a day of it if I took my time and did everything just so.

First off, though, I'd tidy up the place, make the bed, pick up clothes, that kind of thing so I wouldn't look like I'd been abandoned without a hint in the world of how to fend for myself. The bedroom was a mess, all crowded with things people use — an open powder box spilled on the dresser, the mirror tilted lop-sided, Bethany's earbobs in a jumble on the scarf, one highheel shoe on its side, the other ready to step into. The bed pillows were tossed around except for the one on Bethany's side. There was a strand of black hair on it and a hollow place where her head had been. I could see her sleeping there.

I wished I'd stopped her. I could have if I'd tried hardly at all. I could of gone out on the porch and told Charlotte she woke up sick. There were a lot of things I could of said. Goddamn, I should of done it, too.

I picked up her gown off the bed and put my face in it. I could smell myself on it along with her powdery scent. The arms smelled like her skin in the hot summer time, slightly off but sweet, like some strange fruit you'd have to get used to.

Right that minute she was on the road to Somersville. Charlotte was more than likely telling her the news from town, all what she was missing not being down at the bank. Or maybe they were singing. The Malones knew every number in the hymnbook and a lot of other songs I never heard of. They were forever singing Irish tunes Rowe taught them or sometimes ones we learned at school like "Grandfather's Clock" and "Skinamarink" and "The Band Played On." Back then I never sang at all, not even when the teacher said I'd get a whipping if I didn't. I knew that song, though — that "Casey would waltz with a strawberry blond and the band played on."

I pressed the gown to my face and hummed a little. I could hear Miss Letchworth at the old upright pounding out the tune in assembly. "But his brain was so loaded it nearly exploded, the poor girl would shake with alarm. He'd ne'er leave the girl with the strawberry curls and the band played on."

Now that was a damn strange song. I lay back on the bed, the gown still over my face. I should of gone with them. I knew I did a lot that wasn't right. I left her home too much, just like she said. Well, hell, I married this beautiful girl I couldn't keep my hands off of and then all a sudden she's this waddling cow with fat ankles and, goddammit, a face as round and dull as a washpan. Still, I put that baby there.

I knew she was laughing and singing and feeling good with her folks. They'd suck her back in if they got half a chance. Goddamn, I should of gone so I could keep her to myself. I ought to get in the truck and catch up with them. I would do it if I wasn't too tired to move.

When I woke up, it was afternoon and somebody was banging on the door.

ED

Annette and me were going to Wilson's Beach about three and knowing Joel was over there by his lonesome, I thought we'd take him with us. When I got him roused, he stumbled out on the back porch looking groggy and slow as a old hound.

"I got things to do," he told me.

But I kept after him. "You been sawing logs is all. Come on and have a little fun. I hear there's a good band out there tonight."

By evening, he was pretty drunk. I don't reckon he'd put a thing in his stomach all day and by the time I got him to eat a bite it was too late. I tell you the truth, Annette was right disgusted with the both of us so I left him sitting there on the edge of the dance floor, out of harm's way, and got to dancing with her. Keeping the peace, mind you. Well, next thing I know, he's missing. Maybe taking a leak or something, so I dance awhile longer but come time for us to go and he's still off somewhere.

I found him on the beach stretched out on the sand with his pants half off. I got him straightened up best I could and put him in the truck. He hardly come to all the way home.

JOEL

There was this girl, I remember that much. She was shorter than Bethany because her head rested on my chest in a different place when we danced. She smelled like river water and bourbon but underneath there was a musty odor like coal oil. Well, she was a farmgirl, the kind that comes with a bunch of girls to Wilson's Beach of a Saturday night. She had big hands, all calloused, and dry hot skin. We danced awhile — well, mostly we sort of struggled together because I wasn't too sturdy on my feet and she was the kind that just swayed and rubbed against a man, like she was offering more than just a dance, if you understand my meaning.

After awhile I bought us Coca-Colas and we went down to the water. She knew where there was a bottle of liquor buried under the pier and she found it and poured some in our Coca-Cola bottles till they were full again. Then we walked down the beach a ways. When we were just about out of sight of the Pavilion lights, she dropped down on the sand.

"You got a dollar?" she asks me.

"Sure." That's about all I did have.

"Let's see it."

I took a dollar out of my wallet and waved it at her. She took it right out of the air and stuck it in the neck of her dress. Then she patted the sand next to her.

Lying there, I could feel the sand slip under my shirttail and crawl down my neck. My zipper made a little moaning sound. Damn. That's all I remember.

🌺 BETHANY

It was like I'd been away a long time. The house didn't seem familiar, like I was dreaming instead of walking as carefully as I could, trying not to wake him up. I was afraid I'd bump something because all of a sudden I couldn't remember the arrangement of the furniture. There was no moon. Caroline was sleeping so I found the cradle with my foot and put her down. Then I slipped out of my clothes in the dark. When I got into bed, he was awake. "How was it?" he asked me. So I wasn't dreaming after all.

🌺 JOEL

I'd worked all that afternoon, trying to get things ready for her. I was hungover bad. I fried myself six eggs and drank a pot of coffee before I could halfway move. Then I washed myself and my clothes and got them on the line. After that, I worked on what needed fixing. At suppertime I ate soda crackers and catsup and took a stiff drink to wash it down. Just before dark I went out and got the clothes off the line. When I shook my pants, dry sand fell out of the pockets.

There wasn't anything left to do but go on to bed. Outside Amos and a stray started menacing each other, making noise as human as a baby. I threw my shoe at the wall and they moved off, growling deep and mournful. Then I went on to sleep.

What roused me was the headlights of the car and the squawking car door. Then I heard her in the hall, just a rustling sound. She was barefooted. I could see her a little, the pink dress with the sleeves rucked up, the skirt wrinkled deep where she'd sat so long. There was a limp white flower holding her hair back. She put the baby down and the cradle rocked once or twice. She was feeling around for her gown. Her back was white and I could see the side of her tit fall free before she slid under the covers.

"Tell me how it was." I kissed her shoulder. She smelled like the baby.

"It was nice." She put the back of her hand against my cheek.

"Tell me."

"Well, at the reception they had wine punch and finger sandwiches and a cake on a pedestal with a little china bride and groom on top. There was dancing and a toast and everything." She sighed. "But the best part was the wedding itself, when they said their vows — why, it was like I was hearing all that for the first time. Oh, I wish you'd been there! Those words are full of such wonderful promises, and today I felt the meaning of them in my heart. I truly did. I saw our whole life stretching out in front of us. What's here and now is not everything, Joel. It's just a little moment in all the time we have."

Her hair fell across my face when she rested her head on my chest. We went to sleep like that.

Chapter Fifteen

 JOEL

I had to come home every morning at 8:30 to get her to work on time. I'd be sticky with tobacco juice. Sweaty, too. Sometimes she had to nurse the baby while I drove. When we got to the bank, she'd reach over and kiss me hard, like she didn't mind I was dirty.

She was all fixed up. Lipstick, rouge, all that stuff I hated her to wear. It made her look like somebody I didn't know, not like the girl at the depot or the basketball player I loved to watch. Good God, my throat used to get tight when the ball slipped through the net and the crowd roared up. Whoosh, I'd think, she's mine!

In early July we got ten solid days of rain. Looked like the tobacco was drowned, the water stood so deep. Streets in town flooded, too. I know Charlotte's did because Bethany had to take her dinner and eat at the bank. She couldn't get the carriage through the mud for several days.

🌹 MILLY

I was getting a permanent wave. It was a little after noon and Bernice had me hooked up to those metal rods so I looked like I was in the clutches of a great big old spider. The whole place stank of waving lotion so I don't know why a soul would want to come in the place, but I heard the screen door slam and there stood Bethany behind the baby carriage. I'd been as near asleep as you can get under that contraption but I woke right up to speak.

"Well, look who's come for a visit," I said, which caused Bernice to hurry up front from where she was eating a hot dog behind a little curtain in the back. She'd offered to get me one from the sandwich shop but I said no, I'll wait. The truth is I'm not putting one of those things in my mouth until I'm sure what's in it. Lord only knows what it might be.

Anyway, Bethany was looking around at the pictures Bernice has pinned everywhere. They get real faded but Bernice doesn't seem to notice things like that. The girls in the pictures had short hair. It was all the rage then.

"Well, goodness gracious, look at this sweet baby." Bernice smiled down into the carriage. It hadn't occurred to either of us that Bethany might have come on business.

"How much longer under here, Bernice?" I asked her. You feel like a fool attached to that thing, even in front of your nearest and dearest, which Bethany certainly is.

Bernice was talking baby-talk. "You've still got a while. Yes, she does," she cooed to Caroline. "Lucky for your mama, she'll never have need of a old permanent wave, no she won't, not with that hair of hers. I bet you won't either, you precious thing."

"I've been thinking about getting it cut," Bethany said. "It's so muggy these days and with Caroline and all, it's just too much trouble."

Well, you could of knocked me over with a feather. Bernice, too. She raised up out of the carriage and just stared. We were both hoping this was just a passing fancy.

"Lord have mercy, honey, don't ask me to do that!" Bernice said.

Bethany was looking at one of the pictures, a pretty girl with short hair curved at her cheek and her neck exposed. "I like that one," she said.

"Oh, that wouldn't work on you," Bernice said. "That girl's got good hair, mind you, but it's straight as a stick. Every night she rolls it around these new little spongy things and sleeps that way, most likely with a hairnet on."

"I don't believe Joel would like that hairnet a bit. I've yet to see one that's flattering," I said, trying to distract her a little. She was looking at the bottles and combs and such lined up on Bernice's counter. I could see through the mirror how serious she was.

"Well, then, what else can you do?"

"Why, I couldn't do a thing, honey! Not a thing! It won't grow back overnight, you know!"

"I certainly do hope not," Bethany said.

Well, I've seen her like that before so I thought we might as well give up. About then the screen door popped open again and it was Charlotte. She waved at me, then wanted to know what Bethany was doing in there.

"I'm getting my hair cut. It's so hot and everything."

Anybody who knows Charlotte Woodard would say she'd put up a fight. I know her about as well as anybody and so I just about fell out of my seat — would have if I hadn't been attached to that machine — when she said, "Why, I think that's a marvelous idea. You need to look mature if you're going to make your mark in business." With that, she started rocking the carriage with her foot. "Bernice, we went to Traxler's wedding over in Lenoir County recently and I tell you the truth, every lady there young through middle-age had short hair. It makes young women look older and women of a certain age look younger. Why, Bethany and Lizzie were the only ones over sixteen with long hair in the whole place. Even Lucille, who's trying her best to keep Lizzie an infant, commented on it."

"But Charlotte —" Bernice started.

I knew better than to say a word.

"It's up to her, Bernice. I'm just passing. But I did think you'd be interested in how people are looking elsewhere."

"Well, I reckon I am," Bernice said, "but —"

Before she could finish, Bethany had plopped herself right down in the chair. "I want it cut," she said like she'd just that minute gotten aggravated with the entire world. "I want you to do it right now."

Well, Bernice put the sheet around her but she looked as grim as I've ever seen her, including that time she singed Hazel Watson's hair clear to the roots. Charlotte was beaming and Bethany was looking at herself in the mirror hard, like this was going to be her last look. I do believe Bernice's scissors were shaking in her hand, else they were clicking like she was trying to practice some. Nobody said another word till the job was done.

"Oh, oh, oh," I cried out, "I can't believe it. Why, Bethany, you look like another person!"

Charlotte was holding the bundle of hair she'd been collecting off the floor. "Yes, she does, doesn't she?" She was as satisfied as the cat that got the cream.

Of course, by then Bernice had let me stay too long and I had frizz but it was worth it. I wouldn't trade being there for anything in the world.

🌸 JOEL

Somebody I didn't know was bringing my baby out of the bank, somebody with hair shorter than mine. When she got closer I could see, even with mud caked on the windshield, that it was her. She swung up into the truck with Caroline on her shoulder and shut the door. I revved up the engine but we didn't go anywhere.

"I'm ready," she said to me.

"I'm waiting for my goddamn wife," I told her.

"Let's just go," she said. "I'll tell you about it at home."

I shook the wheel so hard the truck rattled. "You cut your goddamn fucking hair," I yelled. I didn't care who heard. "You just went and did it, goddammit."

"It was so much trouble, what with work and the baby," she said. "Anyway, it's my hair."

I made the truck jump into reverse and we squealed off down the street. "Shut up," I told her. "Just shut the hell up."

BETHANY

He didn't come directly in the house. I went on to the bedroom and put Caroline in her cradle. I rested my hand on her back for a minute because that sometimes soothed her to sleep. Then I looked at myself in the mirror. The heat had curled my hair even more but I still liked it. It will grow, I thought to myself. That's what I'll tell him. In a year, he'll hardly even know I cut it. Besides, it's my hair.

But what was truly mine? My cheek where his knuckles sank, was that mine? My stomach where his fist caught under my ribs and jerked me up against the wall? He struck again and my head and shoulder banged so hard on the door jamb I thought I'd been shot. He had a gun. I knew that.

"It's my hair," I screamed at him. "It's mine!" Then blood and vomit filled my mouth. It gurgled and choked in my throat like I was being strangled.

When I came to, he was holding me. At first, I didn't know why I was on the floor but then I felt raw and sticky and there was a stench on me. Bile burned up in my throat again but I managed to push it down.

"Thank God you're all right," he was crying close to my face. I'd never seen him truly cry before and he looked ugly with it, like it had gnarled his face. "I get crazy sometimes. I don't know, God, something comes over me. I get so hot inside and I have to let it out. I have to." His face was red and wet. "But you're all right. It's not bad. You're fine."

I lay there too scared to move. I felt broken inside. I thought all my bones were crushed and my heart was about to stop. There was blood trickling down my neck. I wanted to die. I remember thinking how simple it would be, how easy. It wouldn't hurt much, not like this. Mama was dead and wasn't she happy there, leaning on heaven's gate waiting for people she knew? Weren't all the little babies in the world who had died there? Young soldiers and grandmothers? Girls in white dresses singing lullabies?

Then I heard a wail, my baby awake and needful. I pulled myself up out of his arms and stumbled against the dresser. Caroline was squirming and fussing so I tried hard to get my bearings. It hurt to breathe and I wiped the blood off my cheek with my sleeve. Then I went to take care of what was mine.

❀ CHARLOTTE

Do you think he could hide the truth from me? Why, I didn't believe for one minute she had a stomach ache. Bethany's had an iron constitution all her life except when she was first pregnant and I knew she wasn't pregnant again, not nursing regular like she was. I didn't question Joel though, let him stand right there in the kitchen and lie to my face while I shucked corn for dinner.

"I just went by the bank and told Mr. Watson," he said, "then I got to thinking you might pass by and worry, not seeing her there." Just like he gave a lick what I thought about anything. Well, I thought, let's just give you time to get back in the field where you belong and I'll see for myself. I waited all of thirty minutes before I went.

She came to the kitchen door so I was looking at her

through the screen. There was a deep shadow across her body but I could tell she was holding herself wrong with her face turned away.

"He said you were sick." I yanked the screen door open.

"It's nothing," she said, backing off.

"Let me see your face." I touched her chin to turn her head and she grimaced. Her cheek and temple were bruised and the corner of her eye was swollen shut. "Oh, God. He did this!" I tried to take her in my arms but she pulled away, gasping. "Where else?" I asked her. "Where else are you hurt?"

"Here," she said, touching her rib cage. "It was because I cut my hair. I mean, it's like that's all he cared about. My hair, Charlotte! My hair!" She was sobbing but she sucked back the tears, trying to hold still.

"Go ahead and cry," I told her.

"I can't. It hurts too much. It hurts every time I breathe."

"I tried to tell you, Bethany. Nobody strikes out once and stops there. It's like a dog killing chickens." I couldn't think what to do. "Maybe you should see Fred."

"I can't go to him," she cried. "He delivered Caroline!"

"He's not going to tell anybody. Listen, you could have broken ribs or worse."

But she wouldn't.

"Well, you've got to get out of here. Come home with me."

"I can't do that."

"To Mama's then. We'll go out there for the day."

"And let her see me like this? You know I can't, Charlotte."

"We'll tell her you fell, you ran into the bedpost in the night. You were hoeing the garden and the hoe came back on you. We'll think of something."

Finally I got her to ride around. Thank goodness, Mena was at home taking care of things. She'd see to the children and get dinner on the table for Mac so I had the better part of the day free. We rode all the way to Lawrence and back, me talking all the time, trying to get her to go to my house. We stopped at a filling station and sat in the car drinking a soft drink while she nursed. It was one of the saddest sights I've ever seen, her beautiful face all bruised and swollen bending over that precious baby. It just about broke my heart.

❧ BETHANY

Dear Livy,

Remember how you said we had to get away from here? You said it till I was sick of it. I remember I couldn't see how being in a strange place could be anybody's ambition. I'd done that, you know, coming to live with Charlotte and Mac and making Whitney my home when I didn't know a soul but my cousins and they were out in the country.

Anyway, we both know I didn't listen. I went on dreaming — and lo and behold, there was Joel standing there looking at me with those eyes! Good heavens, I'm shivering this minute and it's the hot summertime thinking about how he looked at me out in the backyard that morning! Love happens that fast, Livy — I'm living proof of it.

Well, I told you I'd write and tell you all about how we're doing but first I want to thank you for the little comb and brush set you gave Caroline. The next time I get to Lawrence I'm going to have a C engraved on it. You shouldn't have spent all that money but I treasure it — you know I do! When you have a baby, I'll get you something just as nice.

I've been back at the bank a couple of weeks now. Mr. Watson lets me stop and nurse whenever I need to so I've been able to keep my milk. Pretty soon I'll have to start weaning her, though. Milly says when it gets winter, she'll watch her for me. Her little girl, Sarah, keeps her pretty much at home anyway. Charlotte said she will help pay for it and she'll take Caroline when it's inconvenient for Milly. I know I used to talk perfectly terrible about Charlotte but she has been good to me, she and

Mac both, and I hope you'll forget all the things I said if you haven't already.

Charlotte is bossy and all but now I see more than ever how she always meant well. I know I'm grown but when I need something, she's the first person I think of. Before Joel, even.

I should tell you so you don't faint dead away when you come home next — I got my hair cut. It's right at the bottom of my ear and I've gotten the most compliments on it. I need to look more grown up if I'm to have a future at the bank — but more than that, I like the freedom of it. I can wash it in a minute now and brush it dry. Well, it's more than that even — it's one of the only things I've ever done without asking anybody. Bernice didn't want to do it either but she saw I meant business. My heart was pounding and I had to make myself sit still. Then I practically floated back to the bank, my head felt so light. I felt free!

You'll have to know Joel didn't like it. At first he was pretty mad but he's gotten over it now. At least he doesn't mention it. I want to be pretty for him, I really do, but I think I look as good as can be expected until I get rid of these extra pounds. Charlotte says I eat like a bird so it's bound to be nursing fat. When I wean the baby it'll just fall away, to hear her tell it.

I'll miss nursing though. To tell the truth, I like being touched like that. Joel and I — well, Caroline takes a lot of time and with me working all day and him in the fields, we don't get together much lately. He's been sleeping down at the tobacco barns some. He and Ed and J.C. take turns when they've got barns fired up but sometimes I think Joel takes more turns than are fairly his. Olivia, when you start falling in love, I want you to pay attention to a lot of little things — oh, never mind, I don't know what I'm talking about!

The next time you're home, you come to see me, you hear? Are you saving to buy a car? Your mama was in the bank saying you were thinking about it. Oh, guess what! Douglas Watson — who spent the first part of the summer touring around the country in his Packard — is here working in the bank till school starts again. Why don't you come home and marry him!?! Then we can ALL ride around in his automobile! Hugs and kisses, B.

CHAPTER SIXTEEN

✿ MILLY

The postcard Charlotte sent me from their family vacation to Richmond was a picture of an old church with a Civil War monument in front. On the back she wrote: "This trip is just what I needed! Mac's sister is showing us all the sights and the children are thrilled! Today we're going shopping at Thalheimer's!" I stopped in at the bank to show Bethany.

"Thank goodness she's having a good time," Bethany said when she gave the card back. "She's waited long enough."

"Charlotte could travel if she wanted to," I told her. "The truth is she's a homebody."

"Well, I'm not. I love to go places," Bethany said although I couldn't think where she'd ever been. "When we can, Joel and I are going to New York City and ride all the way to the top of the Empire State Building."

"Do what?" It was Douglas Watson. He'd stepped into the cage behind her and was smiling out at me. Together they looked like a handsome framed picture.

"We were just discussing travels," I said, waving the card at him. "Charlotte is having a lovely vacation in Richmond."

"I love to travel myself," Douglas said. He had filled out since high school. His shoulders had broadened so he wore a suit with style and his hair showed improvement, too. It was waving across his forehead just so and sometimes he flipped it backwards with his hand like he knew it had turned out better than we'd expected.

"Douglas and one of his classmates spent the first part of the summer on a trip," Bethany said. "He's been telling me about it."

"We drove out to see America," Douglas said. "Of course, with the dust storms out west we didn't see as much as we'd planned."

"What a wonderful experience!" I told them. "Oh, to be young and carefree!"

"Why, Mrs. Holmes, you are young!" he said.

By then Sarah was fussing so I hurried with my business so I could get her on outside. On the sidewalk I saw Joel waiting under the bank awning. His face was close to the barred window and he was standing as still as stone.

🌸 BETHANY

I knew Joel had seen us together but I didn't intend to feel bad about it. After all, Douglas was a friend from way back and his daddy ran the bank. I had to be nice to him.

"You ready?" Joel had stopped midway across the shiny marble floor. His brogans were dropping little clumps of mud on the tiles and he had an oil stain above the crotch of his pants where he'd leaned under the hood of the truck. One rolled-up sleeve was hanging ragged at his elbow. He looked like a derelict.

"Let me help you," Douglas said at my shoulder. Before I could stop him, he'd lifted Caroline out of the carriage behind me and was taking her around the cages to Joel.

"Good-night," I called out. Phyllis and Jeanette were locking their drawers and collecting their things. Douglas was handing Caroline to Joel. She rolled between them like a sack of meal, then Joel had her against his chest with her little head in the crook of his arm. "Hello, little darling," he said to her. "How's my baby girl?"

"She's as sweet as her mama," Douglas said. "About as pretty, too."

"Douglas is working here till he goes back to school," I said.

"Getting a little headstart," Douglas said. "The business world is pretty tough right now."

"Well, not everybody's got their own bank to practice in," Joel said. Douglas kept on smiling like he didn't see how rude Joel was being.

I just wanted to get away. "I'm ready, sweetheart," I said.

When Douglas settled his hands in his pockets, light flashed on the brass bars of his suspenders. "Good to see you, Joel. Maybe we can go out sometime if I can find a date around here. Bethany was the only girl I ever paid any attention to when we were growing up."

"Why, that's not true," I said. "You dated Nell Bishop our whole senior year."

"Because I'd given up on you," Douglas said.

Outside, I took the baby from Joel and got in the truck. "Look how the sun puts a reddish cast on her hair," I said. "Why, Joel, she's going to look just like you. Joel?"

But he didn't say anything, just started the truck and pulled away from the curb. Right then something in his profile touched me. Beneath his tight jaw, his squinting eye, his lips pressed hard, I saw the little boy he'd been, his angel face, and I felt this welling up inside, this longing to have known him then, to have held him in my arms. I wanted to have loved him just like I loved Caroline, to have taken him into my heart when he needed it most. Well, I thought, it's not too late.

Hadn't he told me once I'd saved him? It was a long time

ago, last summer before morning sickness and my heavy shape, when we'd been together every night and he'd said all kinds of things in the dark, words he'd never bring himself to say in daylight. I'd felt more than love for him then, more than passion. It was tenderness I'd felt.

At home, I nursed Caroline as quickly as I could and started supper while Joel washed at the pump on the back porch. Once when the glint of the mirror caught my eye I went to the door and looked out at his back, how his muscles moved under his skin as he lathered his face. It was the razor held lightly between his fingers that made me turn away.

After supper, I sat at the table staring at a book Charlotte had lent me but my mind kept shifting to Joel who was leaning against the porch post smoking. He stood there a long time before he disappeared around the house. I listened for the truck starting up but everything was quiet.

What was he thinking? I wondered. My hand trembled on the page. I heard his footsteps on the porch, then the screen door creaking open. I closed the book carefully, my fingers tight on the binding.

"Look," he said, holding a blur of red in front of me. It was the first tomato from our garden.

JOEL

She had on a heavy gown and it was the hot summertime. I was naked like usual.

"Don't go to sleep," I said.

She turned over on her back. "Do you want to talk?" she asked me.

I started nuzzling her neck. Licked at her earlobe. "About what?"

"About today. About Douglas."

"I don't give a shit about Douglas." I rested my arm across

her. I could feel her tit through the gown. "I just care about you."

"I care about you, too," she said.

I put a lot of little kisses along her jaw, working to her lips.

"I'll always love you," she said just before I sunk my tongue deep into her mouth.

I fumbled with her gown. She was hidden in it. Then I felt it give, a tear like a little cry, and her bosom spilled out. Her arms were caught in the sleeves and I reckon her feet were all tangled in the bottom but I didn't care. I came over her like a sheet of fire, burning hot and smoking like that.

"Come," I cried in her ear. "Come!"

🌹 BETHANY

But I couldn't. I felt trapped — no, more than that — it was like a deep shiver that stopped just on the edge of feeling, like even though my skin was burning, inside I was ice. When he lifted away, I felt cold everywhere.

I gathered my torn gown around me as best I could and turned on my side. Through the window I could see one bright star as cold as a jewel in the sky. How long would it live, I wondered, because I knew stars died. I'd seen showers. Once Mac and I even climbed on top of the house and lay on a blanket on the roof for hours while the sky sparkled and danced with dying stars.

Remembering, I sighed deep inside, then heard it escaping.

"What?" Joel said in a fog of sleep and rolled against me like a stone.

I don't think I dreamed unless the star showers were a dream. Before dawn I awoke thinking I'd heard Caroline. I lay there listening with my eyes closed but she was quiet. The sheet was still crammed at the footboard and Joel was gone. I knew without looking.

I heard a click. I opened my eyes without moving and tried to find shapes in the dark — the cradle against the wall, the dresser with the top drawer hanging open, the starless sky at the window. Then I saw him cross in front of the window and drop beside the bed. I could feel the gun near my head, knew without seeing how his hand cupped the handle, his finger curled at the trigger. I didn't move.

Don't, I said in my head. Don't do this. I didn't breathe. My breath held so long in my chest tickled, then ached. I guess it was like drowning. Little splinters of light struck behind my eyes. Was I already shot?

Then the bed trembled a little. He was moving away. I followed his movement across the room. He was naked and his back and buttocks glided in and out of the shadows. I heard the drawer closing softly. Then he slumped against the dresser and his face came into the first pale light of morning. It was a face I'd never seen before, a child's face full of terror so deep he could have been paralyzed with it. I knew this was not the first time such a thing had happened.

Chapter Seventeen

BETHANY

When Joel took me to work the next morning there were already people on the street: Myrtle Walker waiting for the bank to open; Mr. Bronson rolling out his awning; a gang of little boys passing with worm cans and cane poles. I started to get out without kissing him. I had Caroline in one arm and the baby bag caught under the other.

"Hey, gimme a kiss," he said so I leaned over as best I could and kissed him on the cheek.

"Wait a minute," he said but I pretended I didn't hear.

Douglas came to let me in. He took Caroline's bag off my shoulder, stopped to remind Mrs. Walker that it wasn't quite nine yet, then locked the door behind us. I knew Joel saw but I didn't care.

I barely had Caroline down when Douglas unlocked the door again and let Mrs. Walker in.

"Why, Bethany, you're as pretty as a picture," she said without even looking. "I saw you getting out of that truck a minute ago with that precious little baby and I thought to myself, Why, she ought to be getting out of a fine convertible car, not that old thing." She cocked her head toward Douglas at his desk like she was recommending him. "Well, I've got business with Doug this morning. I hope he's here."

"Yes Ma'am, he is. Douglas, Mrs. Walker's here to see your daddy and I — I —" They were both staring at me so I know I must have been a sight.

"Go on in, Mrs. Walker," Douglas said. "Bethany, what is it?" He was separating the morning mail between his fingers but, looking at me, he let it drop in a heap on his desk.

"I need to see Mac," I said. "I'll run if I can just go this minute."

"I'll take you in the car," he said.

"No, but I need to leave Caroline here. I won't be gone long."

"Go on then," he told me.

I ran as far as I could, until I had to stop and bend double to get my breath. Then I ran again. I ran all the way.

🌸 MAC

Her dress looked damp and sticky with dust when she got here. She burst in like something was after her and leaned against the door panting and heaving. She looked terrible.

"Thank God you're here! I don't know what I'd of done." She had her hands crossed on her chest, like that would help her get her breath.

"What is it, honey?" I got up and started to her, but something stopped me. It was like she couldn't be touched yet.

"Tell me, Beth."

"This morning when I woke up, he was holding a gun to my head," she said.

"Oh, God." I went to hold her then. She was trembling.

"What am I going to do?" she sobbed into my shoulder.

I kept on holding her. "You'll come stay with us. You can't

go back out there."

"Charlotte will be so mad." She tried to straighten herself up. "She'll say she told me so."

"No, she won't. She loves you."

"I can't be at the bank when he comes to get me. I can't."

"I know. I'll see to it at noon. I'll talk to Doug and we'll work something out. I don't think you should be down there at all until this is resolved. We can keep you safe at home."

"I've got to go back this morning. I just left, Mac. I ran all the way here. I didn't know what to do!"

Her broken face made me want to cry myself. "You did the right thing. Now I'll walk you back to the bank and at noon I'll come get you and take you home. Do you think you can get through the morning down there?"

She nodded and took the handkerchief I offered her.

"The baby's all right, isn't she?"

"She's fine." She tried to smile. "He'd never hurt her," she said.

🌺 JOEL

I knew something was wrong the minute I pulled up at the bank. Well, hell, I knew it ever since she gave me that little pecking kiss that morning. God, there were times that first summer when I had to push her off because she was making herself late to work smooching on me. It got different though.

All day I thought about her. We were priming and I knew before night I'd be hanging from the rafters, getting the barn in — I had the steadiest legs among us — but between times, I'd see her a few minutes while we had a bite of supper.

At quarter of five, I dropped my tobacco in the mule truck at the end of the row and left the field, stopping just to douse my head in the rain barrel under the shelter and take a drink from the water jug Daddy left there.

At five I was waiting in front of the bank. A little after, the other tellers came out. They huddled in the doorway for a minute before breaking out into the sunshine. Beth wasn't with them. Before long Douglas came to the door and pulled the shade down.

"What the fucking hell?" I said loud enough for a woman on the street to hear. She grabbed ahold of her little kid and hurried on.

I backed the truck out into the street. Damn if I was going up there banging on the door asking Douglas Watson where my wife was. I thought maybe she was sick. I'd go to Milly's since Charlotte was supposed to be on that vacation we'd be hearing about till kingdom come. Then again, maybe she was back home by now.

The baby carriage was parked on the front porch. I rested my hand on the handle while I waited for somebody to answer the door. It was Mena. She was twisting a rag and refusing to look at me.

"I've come to get my wife," I said to her through the screen.

"Miss Charlotte's comin," Mena said. "She be here directly."

"I don't want to talk to Charlotte." I rattled the screen door. It was hooked. "It's Bethany I've come for."

"Well, she's not leaving here," Charlotte said. I could see Mena backing down the hall. "She's staying with us from now on. I just got back from out there getting her things."

"You went in my house? You bitch!" I didn't care who heard me.

"You're not hurting me," Charlotte said. "Or Bethany either. Not anymore. It's over with."

I yelled then. I didn't intend to because I knew she'd see it as weakness but I couldn't help myself. "Bethany! Beth-a-ny!"

"Give her two weeks," Charlotte said. "That's what she's asking for. Two weeks here with us without you bothering her so she can decide what to do. We know about the gun, Joel. She told us how she woke up with you pointing it at her."

"I'll bring it to her," I said. "She can have it. I don't know why I ever bought it. It was crazy —"

"You're right about that," Charlotte said.

"I have to talk to her. Give me five minutes." I knew I was begging but I didn't care. I thought if she saw me she'd want to come home. "She's got our baby," I said.

"And thank God for that," Charlotte said. "If you want to communicate with her, leave a message with Mac. Or write her a letter. But don't come here again until she sends for you." She had her hand on the door, ready to close it. "I'm not letting her out of my sight, Joel. I promise you that. You'll have to walk across me to get to her."

The door shut hard. I went to Lawrence instead of going home. Somebody else could get the fucking tobacco in.

🍂 BETHANY

When he called out, I had to clamp my hand over my mouth to keep from answering. Then I heard the truck leave. Charlotte came up to check on me but I guess she could tell I wasn't going to talk to her so she left me alone. Besides, she didn't want to hear how mixed up I was when everything was perfectly clear to her.

That night I woke up every few minutes it seemed like. It was like I was startled by the streetlight outside the window or the rumble of a car on the street. I felt like I was in another country.

When Patsy was younger, she used to have night terrors. Sometimes we'd find her in the hall sleepwalking toward the stairs like a little haunt all pale and eerie in her white gown. Once Charlotte found her all the way downstairs at three o'clock in the morning waiting in the kitchen for breakfast. Charlotte took her hand and led her back to bed without a word because Mena said that was the thing to do.

"Don't go worryin them spirits," she said. "Leastways, I wouldn't want them loose in my house."

Maybe Charlotte felt the same about me. Maybe she thought that eventually I'd start feeling comfortable again if she stayed clear and let me be. I didn't though. Even after several days, I was still a stranger there and I'd wake up panicked, thinking I'd missed an important event or that somebody'd been calling me a long time but I'd just heard.

I'd lie there with my heart pounding and mouth parched, listening for Caroline's breathing. Sometimes I'd get up and touch her, just a fingertip on the back of her curled hand or my palm against her diapered bottom. I had to resist an urge to pick her up and hold her, even bring her in the bed with me. I wanted to whisper in her tiny ear, "I will love you forever and ever. You are everything to me."

I knew there was a chance I'd be raising her alone from then on but I didn't want to think about it. I was giving Joel time like Charlotte and Mac said but I didn't know what good it would do, not without somebody to help him. Nobody but me knew what he was like. I was the only one he loved enough to strike.

CHAPTER EIGHTEEN

BETHANY

If Charlotte wouldn't go out in the country and see about Amos, I'd go myself. I wanted the cat with me.

"But I don't even like cats and they don't like me either," she complained. "How am I suppose to catch a cat?"

"With a can of sardines," Mac said. "Or this piece of chicken."

We had just finished dinner and there was one leg left on the plate.

"I'm not giving my good fried chicken to a cat!" Charlotte started collecting the dishes.

"Well, you'd better take something to encourage him." Mac went back to his paper. "I don't think you'll catch him otherwise. Try some catnip."

"What?" Charlotte was already distracted.

"What? Hell, woman, pay attention!" He was laughing before she slapped down his paper.

"I declare, I don't know what's come over you, Mac." She was laughing, too. "I'm starting to think having a baby in this house has perked you up some."

"Maybe so, but don't you go getting any ideas." He grabbed her around the waist and pulled her down in his lap. "I feel like I'm Caroline's grandpa. We're too old for a baby. Isn't that right, Beth?"

"We are not," Charlotte said. "Why, almost all the women I know older than me are still having babies. Miss Addie Suggs had a baby when she was fifty."

"Miss Addie Suggs was slow-witted. I wouldn't think you'd want to be following after her." Mac squeezed her hard and put a smacking kiss on her neck.

This is how marriage is supposed to be, I thought. I saw as clear as day that this was what I'd expected with Joel. I laughed with them but inside my stomach grabbed and a weight pressed on my heart. See this, Joel, I said in my head. See how happy we can be.

"Mac, you go get the cat." Charlotte was nuzzling his neck.

"I don't have time this afternoon. I swear I don't."

"I'll go," I told them. "I said I would."

"And I said absolutely not." Charlotte pulled free of Mac and went back to clearing the table. "I'll do it myself," she said.

❀ CHARLOTTE

Of course, I couldn't find Amos. I stood beside the car calling "kitty, kitty" like a fool. I didn't want to go near the house but finally I walked close enough to see that the chipped dish and water bowl Bethany always left on the back porch were gone. So now he was starving a cat.

I got back in the car and pulled onto the road. Then it occurred to me I might as well go on over to the Calders and see if Amos was there. At least that might stop Bethany from coming to look.

The house was closed up as usual. Even in the hot summertime, it looked empty and lifeless. No wonder the boy was crazy as a loon. Maybe all of them were. A boarding house had more to recommend it than that place did.

Just as I got out, a wind came up bringing a low, churning cloud of dust across the cotton field and, by the time I got to the porch, the grit was stinging my arms and legs. J.C. must have heard me drive up because he came out to meet me. He practically lifted me out of the dust cloud.

"Just a little hint of what must be going on out west," he said. "I tell you what's the truth, I'd hate to be one of them folks out in Oklahoma. None of us around here's got much, but at least we can see to get to it."

"That's true." I slapped at my skirt. My mouth felt gritty when I bit down. "As a matter of fact, I was thinking along those lines just this morning — how we ought to see to what's ours."

"You've come about Joel, I reckon." J.C. was frowning below the brim of his broken straw hat. "I know she's left him. It was brought up to me in town this morning and I had to act like I knew about it."

The air went still again and I brushed my hand through my hair, fixing myself right in front of him.

"Actually, I came looking for Bethany's cat. She's been worried sick about him. We all know Joel never cared a thing about that cat."

"Well, Amos is here as much as he's any place," J.C. said. "Emma feeds him. He's a tom, you know, so he visits around. We watch out for him, though."

"I'll tell her that. It'll rest her mind some." I was relieved I didn't have to bring the cat home.

"You tell her he's fit as a fiddle." J.C. looked out at the field like he was thinking. "I've been wondering if I should go have a talk with Bethany myself. I couldn't decide. You never know when it's best to let things be."

Well, spare us the sight of you in the parlor, I thought. "I'd be glad to take her a message," I told him.

"I reckon that might be best." He straightened up like he had a speech to make. "You tell her I know Joel's not easy to live with, but I believe he truly loves her and that baby of theirs. The day Caroline was born, he came over here and just about cried over the pain he'd caused — her labor and all. You tell her he's a growing boy still, with wild buck ways about him but it's best to forgive and forget if she can."

"I don't know about that. How can you say he's not dangerous?" He didn't answer so I thought I might as well have my say. "He hit her, J.C., and not just once. Several times."

He looked struck himself. He leaned on the porch railing, his face turned away but I could see the muscles in his neck working like he was trying to swallow.

I went on: "Then, the night before she came to us, she woke up and he was right there by the bed holding a gun to her head." The truth is I didn't care if I hurt him. He didn't matter any more than a gnat to me.

"Jesus!" He slammed the flat on his hand on the railing. "God help us, I didn't think he'd do anything like that. That's the truth, Charlotte."

"Well, you were wrong." I swatted at a bee that had buzzed onto the porch and was menacing me. "I'll tell her you're seeing after Amos."

At the car, I turned back and said, "You give Emma my best."

He nodded but I knew he was wounded. I turned the car down the lane and let it buck and jump however it wanted to. I was too worn out to care.

🌺 JOEL

I saw the car bumping down the road. Charlotte was leaning over the wheel looking all fired up. She'd been out to Daddy's so I reckon he knew all I hadn't told him.

All week I'd been doing like usual. All anybody wanted from me was two hands and a strong back, anyhow. There wasn't much talk under the barn shelters, not in the field either. It was too hot. Sweat dripped in our eyes and the only times we came in was to swish our heads in the water barrel and get a cool drink. Ed didn't try his usual horsing around and the women under the shelter didn't pay us any mind. I didn't even tease old Mary who worked in the house for Mama in the wintertime. She could still tie so fast we could hardly see her hands, just the quick flutter of the leaves dropping to either side of the stick without a single broken stem.

So the only voice I heard was Beth's. A soft breath at my ear. Words I couldn't make out. She'll come back, I'd think. Bent low in the hot sun, I'd think that.

Night was different. I had nightmares so bad I got to where I dreaded sleep. One night I dreamed I was hanging by a piece of twine that was slowly unwinding through the sky. All a sudden, a light zoomed out of the dark — Charlotte brandishing a hot white sword, her face afire. "Aha!" she screamed and broke the string with one stroke. I was falling when I woke up.

I wrote this letter: "My darling Beth, you are my life, my heart. I have thrown the gun away. J."

When I handed it to Miss Trudy at the post office, she tested in on her palm like it weighed too much, then said, "Well, Joel, you ought to deliver this yourself."

"I'm mailing it," I told her. "Anyway, you're not supposed to look at the mail."

"Well, I have to see what box to put it in," she said, all in a huff. "The fact is I don't remember two seconds later."

But I knew she did. By mid-afternoon I reckon it was all over town that I sent a letter to my wife at the Woodards. Now that Charlotte had come snooping around, Daddy knew it, too.

🌿 J.C.

All afternoon I'd been having a bad ache in my chest but when I saw Joel clomping down the cotton row toward the house, I went out and waited on him. "You stay for supper," I said to him. "I don't reckon you've been eating right all week."

"I can rustle up something when I have to," he told me.

"Well, doggone it, boy, if you behaved yourself, you wouldn't have to!"

"I saw Charlotte was here."

"She came looking for the cat but she had plenty to say."

"I hate that bitch." He dug in his shirt pocket for his Camels and offered the pack to me. I didn't take one but he lit up. "She'll come back, Daddy," he said. "She won't keep my baby away from me long."

"I never thought a son of mine would hit a woman," I said to him. "You sure as hell won't raised that way." My arm was trembling some but I held onto it with my other hand so he wouldn't notice.

"You're right about that." He was squinting in the smoke. "I can't say I was hardly raised at all."

"Now boy, you can't go blaming this on a soul but yourself. When a man puts up his hand, he's responsible for where it lands."

"It'll never happen again, Daddy. She knows that."

I could see then how bad he felt. I put my arm around him so we were standing shoulder to shoulder, looking out across the dry yard together. I could hardly hold onto him, my side felt so weak. Heat was hanging above the vents of the tobacco barn we'd fired up the night before. "You stay and eat, you hear," I said. "I won't say nothing about this to your mama."

"I don't know as she'd care anyhow," he said.

JOEL

After supper, I went back over to the house. Amos was there so I searched in the pie safe and found some moldy corn-bread for him. Poured milk over it and set it out on the porch. He ate, then came mewing around my legs. I rubbed him a little, then went on inside and closed the door. In the bedroom, I stripped and lay down on the bed. I stank but I didn't care. Maybe I'd wash later.

Right then I wanted Bethany. I needed her. Five minutes with her and she'd remember how she loved me, how I could make her feel with my mouth and hands. I wondered what she was doing, there with all those people around her. She wasn't thinking about me at all. I'd know if she was. I'd feel it.

I got up and went to the dresser where the gun was deep in the top drawer. It gleamed in my hand. I liked touching it and so I sat on the edge of the bed for a long time feeling it get warm in my hand. Holding it, I felt better.

Chapter Nineteen

🌸 BETHANY

Charlotte said the house where I lived with Daddy was in the mill district, huddled right up against colored town. She said it hurt her so bad to see me and Mama living there. That's why she couldn't stand for me to be in J.C.'s little tenant house although the truth is that's how a lot of people get started — staying on the homeplace however they can. There's no shame in it.

Charlotte said my daddy lost the house a long time ago and was living over in Lawrence in a room above the Lyric Theater where I've been to the show a hundred times. Maybe he was sitting up there by himself while I was below watching whatever picture Charlotte wanted to see. Now Joel was by himself, too, and I was surrounded by people but alone.

I'm grateful for my family, I truly am, but there was just one thing I wanted and that was Joel and me together and everything all right. I wanted to believe in him. I thought he'd scared himself as much as he'd scared me. I thought I knew how he felt.

Charlotte kept telling me I had Caroline to think about. "You're a mother now, not some wide-eyed girl who can afford to take risks," she said. "If there was just you to think about, I'd say give him another chance, I really would. But there's your child to consider."

It occurred to me she was using Caroline to get her way but I didn't want to think that. Charlotte was smart and determined and clear-headed while I wavered from minute to minute. I could still see us in a fairy tale if I wanted to.

MENA

I's sweepin the porch when he come lookin hang-dog, wantin to see her. He don't beg or nothin, says right straight out I's aimin to have a word with my wife. Wants to see the baby, too. I puts the broom down right quick and hooks the screen behind me like Miss Charlotte done told me to do. "You shut the door right in his face," she say but I don't do that. He look kind of helpless. A little ole lost chile.

Miss Charlotte come runnin up to Bethany's room like her coattail's afire.

"He's not setting foot in this house," she says. "I don't care what he said in some letter. Words are cheap, dirt cheap. Actions are what counts."

"He be wantin to see her on the porch," I says. "Her and the baby, too."

"Absolutely not!" Miss Charlotte havin herself a fit now. "Don't do it, honey. Please don't."

But Bethany takes that baby outa the crib and her right warm and sweet-smellin after her bath. Bout half asleep.

"I'll tell him he can come back when Mac's home. We need Mac here," Miss Charlotte says.

"It'll be all right," Bethany says. "I'm just going to speak to him a minute."

Miss Charlotte, she stand in the door, ain't lettin nobody come or go.

"Let me pass," Bethany says. "I love him, Charlotte. That's

what you'll never understand. And he loves me."

Miss Charlotte stare hard in that chile's face like she seein somethin she ain't never seen before, I don't know what. Then she take herself outa the way. "I'll be out there to get you in three minutes," she says.

When Bethany go, Miss Charlotte puts her hands over her face like I never seen her do. It be like she can't stand to see.

🌺 BETHANY

When I first saw him through the screen, he was leaning on the porch railing. He heard me and straightened up. He looked beautiful, so good I know I flushed. I was afraid to say anything. What if the first words I said were I love you? I knew better than that. First I had to be sure of something but I didn't know what exactly. That he'd be faithful and true and tender all the rest of our lives? Maybe that was it.

"I don't want to cause trouble," he said. "I just want to see you and Caroline."

I knew Charlotte was listening. I knew she'd tell me later how this didn't prove anything. Why, you didn't even talk, she'd say. Maybe you don't have anything to say unless it's love-talk, nonsense in a hot, rumpled bed.

I followed him out on the walk to get away from Charlotte. In the sunlight his hair turned golden and the dark muscles in his arms rippled like he wanted to grab me but was managing to stop himself. I stopped, too, at the edge of the step and looked at his face. I could see he expected me to keep coming. He thought all our problems could be solved in one week, with one letter, with one minute of patience on his part.

🌺 JOEL

I heard her lift the hook, then push against the screen with her shoulder and there she was with our baby in her arms. I had on work clothes, clean ones, and I'd thought to polish my shoes. I looked as good as I could and not make a fool of myself. We'd both have laughed if I'd showed up in my wedding suit.

"Oh God, you're here," I said to her.

She just stood there looking flushed. There's never been a prettier sight in the world.

I started toward her, then saw she didn't want that. A shadow came in her eyes. Well, I'd wait and see how it went.

"I got your letter," she said.

"Come out here." I nodded toward the walk and she followed me down. The thing was she stopped with her heels against the bottom step. That's how I knew what was going on.

"I can't come back to you," she said. "Not now, anyway."

"I understand that," I said. "Can I hold her a minute? That's all I want."

🌺 BETHANY

Joel was holding her, swaying slightly like he was lulling her to sleep. He was talking to me, a reasonable conversation I thought considering what I'd just said to him. He wasn't begging, just talking about what was going on out at the farm. I wasn't afraid, but I watched the baby in his arms just like I always watched whatever he held — a starched shirt, a coffee cup he managed to slosh over the rim, a knife rasping across the whetstone.

He stopped talking mid-sentence like his train of thought had been broken. He was looking down at Caroline who was awake in his arms but quiet.

"You are the most beautiful thing I've ever seen," he said softly, so I had to repeat the words in my head before I understood them.

Then he opened his arms. I saw his hands moving, his arms unfolding. I saw the support leave Caroline's head, the quick jerk of her tender neck trying to hold itself straight, the tiny reaching fingers grasping air, but I couldn't move. My baby fluttered slowly like a leaf shunted on the wind.

Oh God, what could a baby fear more than space when she'd spent her whole life so tightly held, her wobbly head in my palm, her face damp with milky heat at my breast? What could her tiny mind reason in those long seconds between her daddy's hands and the pavement? She never cried, never made a sound. The only cry I heard was my own.

When I reached her, blood was trickling from her ear, a thin bright ribbon oozing from a tiny shell. Her body was splayed and loose on the pavement like only her diaper and shirt held her intact. A puddle of blood was spreading out under her. Her little body twitched and her mouth pursed like she was going to suck, then went slack and blue in an instant. Later I knew that was the life going, but at that moment I had hope. When I lifted her against my chest, blood soaked through my clothes like water. Then I felt a surge of milk emptying itself from my breast.

I knew Joel was still there, then I felt him move. I heard the truck door open and I remembered the gun. Maybe he'd shoot me while I knelt there holding our baby. I hoped he would. I wanted to be where Caroline was. The engine started and the truck grumbled and roared away. I was alone.

🌸 CHARLOTTE

The car sputtered like it wasn't going to start but then it caught and we bucked out of the driveway. Mena was on the porch holding onto Patsy who was screaming to go with us.

"Go tell Mac we've gone to the hospital!" I stomped on the clutch and threw the car in gear.

"No! Dr. Frazier's," Bethany screamed at me. She was cuddling the baby who hadn't moved or made a sound since she'd picked her up just minutes ago.

I didn't have time to think, I just turned down Main Street and rammed the car against the curb in front of Fred's office. I left the motor running while I ran in there calling for him.

"That oldest Fletcher girl is having her baby," Gladys started off in that slow monotone she uses to keep people waiting. I reckon I looked like I was ready to pull her up by the throat because then she cried out, "He's gone to the hospital!"

"Call over there and tell him we're coming!" I said.

"What's wrong, Charlotte?" she asked, but I didn't wait to tell her.

The car bounced up on the curb before I could straighten it out, then we were on the road to Lawrence. Only my hands on the wheel kept me in this world. I could feel myself floating away from it, not wanting to be earthbound where such things could happen.

I didn't want to look at Bethany and the baby, then I couldn't help myself. The baby's eyelids and lips were blue and there was a purple swelling at her temple where her soft hair was coming in.

Bethany was looking at her, too. "I told Joel just the other day she's going to look like him, auburn coloring and all. I know you think she's a Malone clear through but she's not. She's Joel's." Her voice was calm, like we were just taking the baby out for a ride.

"We'll be there soon, honey," I said. My hands were shaking. I thought I should have gone by the mill to get Mac. Then he could be driving. But that would mean I didn't have anything to do and I needed something to do.

Bethany was humming softly. It was "My Blue Heaven."

"Just Molly and me and baby makes three, we're happy in my blue heaven," she crooned, then started again, singing all the words until she came to the part about the baby. Right there she broke off.

"That's Joel's favorite song," she said. "When Caroline had the colic so bad, he'd dance around the room with her singing it."

"I didn't know that," I said. I couldn't believe we were having a normal conversation although I suppose that's what a person does at such times. You forget what you're doing because if you remembered, you'd die from it. "I can hardly carry a tune as you well know. When Davey and Patsy were little, I tried singing to them and they fussed even louder. I couldn't even hum to them."

"Oh-h-h-h-h," she cried out like she'd just remembered. "Oh God in heaven!"

We swung in toward the emergency door at the hospital. I pulled up under the portico like I knew what I was doing and honked the horn. Two men came through the swinging doors and dropped off the platform beside the car like they intended to hoist the whole thing up into the hospital.

"It's the baby," I called out and one man swung Bethany's door open and reached in to grab Caroline.

"No!" Bethany screamed at him. "I'll take her." But she let the man help her out and he practically carried her up the ramp while I sat there thinking my heart had stopped. I could feel blood draining out of my head and my vision went blurry. My head bumped on the steering wheel.

"Uh-oh," the other man said. "Don't you go fainting on me."

"I'm all right. Go see about them."

"Don't you worry. Somebody's taking care of that," he said. "I think I'd better give you a hand."

I didn't have any choice but to let him. Inside, he sat me down in a chair. "I've got to find Fred Frazier," I said. "I've got to be with Bethany." I guess I thought I had to hear with my own ears what I already knew.

CHAPTER TWENTY

 JOEL

I had this idea in my head to go see Mama. She'd be surprised to see me in the middle of the day. I drove that way, but
then I didn't turn toward the homeplace after all. Daddy was
across the road bringing a mule out of the field. I could see the
trail of dust they made and then the top of Daddy's hat and that
jaw of his jutting out of its shadow. When I went by, he waved his
hand once like a little salute.

"Good-bye, Daddy," I said to him.

I went on to our house. Everything was the same. Her
mama's dishes were still in the breakfront, all lined up and looking
pretty. Beth had put another plate where one was missing. It was
for the baby and there were little bunnies on it. One day soon
she'd be eating off it. Using that little silver cup Mac's sister sent
her, too. She had all these pretty things and she'd need more. A
little white fur hat and muffler like Beth showed me in a store
window, shoes and dolls and books and wooden puzzles. Well, I
could make toys. I'd just have to get busy whittling again but first
I needed to calm myself down some.

I got the jar of moonshine from behind the sink curtain. It

burned a path clear to my stomach. Didn't go to my heart, though. That's where I was aching, deep in my chest like I'd taken a blow. I went to the bedroom and looked around. The bed unmade like that was a sorry sight so I pulled up the covers and straightened the pillows. It looked better. The dresser top was messy where I'd been going through her things. I used to hold her old slip to my nose trying to smell her on it. Charlotte had left some odds and ends of jewelry, too, and sometimes I'd hold her earbobs in my hand and roll them like marbles till they were warm and sweaty.

I got the gun out of the drawer and put it in my pocket. Then I went out on the front porch. The railing still needed sanding and painting but I could see I wouldn't get to it till fall.

I sat down on the step and looked out toward town. I couldn't see beyond the field and that stand of pines but I knew what it looked like. I could see Coleridge Street and Charlotte's house there on the corner. I could see the porch where Beth and me used to hug and kiss so quiet it felt like ghosts touching.

I could see the walk, too, and her heels tight against the step. I was the one talking. I was the one trying while she stood there holding our baby, what we'd made together. I could see myself reaching out and Caroline coming to my arms. I could feel her on my wrists and arms, how I tightened up to hold her.

The gun was in my hand. I put the muzzle to my chest. I could feel my hands locking over each other and the squeeze of my thumb against the trigger. Light flashed all around me. "Mama," I said and then the bullet struck. It sucked in my chest like I wanted it to, straight for the heart.

❧ DR. FRAZIER

I saw in an instant there was nothing I could do. Bethany was still holding the baby. By then two orderlies and a nurse had tried to take it from her but she refused. At least, somebody had persuaded her to put a blanket around it.

"Help me," she said when I came in. She let me come close enough to open the blanket. I touched the head and felt the crushed fragments beneath the broken skin and then the spongy texture of brain tissue.

"Bethany," I said and put my hand on her hot cheek. She trembled under my fingers. "Honey, she's gone."

"No!" she screamed out and leaned forward, the baby between her breasts and lap, like she was sheltering it.

"Her skull is crushed," I went on because it was all I knew to do. What I know is what I can see and read and reason. Sometimes it doesn't make sense but I have to go ahead with it, anyway. "I think her neck is broken, too. If you'll let me have her a minute —"

"No!" She was shaking all over but she tightened her grip.

Charlotte came in about then. "Bethany, let Fred try to help her!" she cried.

But I shook my head, telling her the truth with my eyes.

🌸 MAC

I found them there in the emergency room: Charlotte and Fred, Bethany holding Caroline.

"Oh, God, he's killed her. He's murdered his own baby," Charlotte screeched at me. Nobody was moving. It was like one of those tableau pictures people make by holding still.

"Mena said there was an accident. I thought she had a little cut or a burn or something." I tried to put my arm around Charlotte but she was too mad to let me hold her.

"He threw her on the cement. I told her not to talk to him. I told her not to let him see the baby. But no, she had to go ahead like she wasn't dealing with a crazy person. I should of locked her up myself, anything to keep her away from him!"

"Charlotte!" Fred got up from his crouch beside Bethany's chair. "I'll get you a sedative. You've got to be strong through this."

"I don't want a sedative. I want him behind bars!" She thrashed in my arms. "Get the police!"

"There's no need." Douglas Watson was in the doorway behind us.

"What is it, Douglas?" I asked him.

"It's Joel." He looked from Charlotte and me to Fred like he needed help but nobody said anything. "It seems his daddy saw him going past a little while ago and something just told him to go on down there and see about him. He found him on the front porch. Bethany, he'd shot himself. He was already dead when his daddy got there."

"Ei-i-i-i-i," she wailed. She was rocking back and forth so hard her head almost touched her knees. The baby was deep in her arms.

"Fred, do something!" Charlotte said.

"What in the world can I do?" Fred said.

"There's not a thing," I said. "Bethany, let Douglas help you up. We're going home now. You bring Caroline and come on."

She let him lift her up. She leaned on him a little, then straightened up. Her face looked empty and flat. "Thank you," she said to Fred who was wiping his eyes under his glasses. "Thanks," she said to Douglas who was guiding her out.

I helped Charlotte along behind them. "We've got two vehicles over here," I said when we were out in the sunlight.

"I'll take care of it," Douglas said. "Daddy and I'll come get your truck after a while." I felt like a big problem had been solved.

I handed Charlotte into the back seat of the Ford. Douglas started putting Bethany in the front but she shook her head until he opened the back door and she slipped in beside Charlotte.

"Let me take her, honey." Charlotte was reaching for the baby.

"No. Can't you see I can't give her up?" she said. So going home, Charlotte held them both.

EMMA

The water was cool. Well, there wasn't reason to heat it. I touched the wadded rag to his cheek. There wasn't hardly any blood on his face. That surprised me some. When J. C. came in to tell me what had happened and how he had Joel wrapped in a blanket on the bed of the truck, I thought about my baby Alice's face, how it blossomed a bloody mass where her little nose and mouth had been. I knew I couldn't look at that again but I didn't say so to J.C.

I stood on the back porch watching him sling our boy over his shoulder and bring him in. I saw the look on his face. I knew then I'd do whatever had to be done to get this over with.

Still I was relieved to see he'd shot himself in the heart and left his face beautiful. Well, he was a handsome boy. Even when he scowled, he had a pretty face. I started cleaning him up, wanting to hurry so his mouth wouldn't set open. I wouldn't have him look like he was crying in his coffin for everybody in town to see — maybe more people than that. Half the county might show up once the news got out.

I could hear J.C. out in the shed. He was planning to make the coffin. He said so while he helped me get Joel laid out on the kitchen table.

"You ought to go out to Rowe Malone's and see what they've got in the shop out there," I told him, wanting to spare him such terrible work. I remember the little coffin he made for Alice, no bigger than a manger and still she looked lost in it before I padded the sides with every scrap of cloth in the house. She looked like a tiny old woman dressed in her snow white baby dress and bonnet. Joel would look all right, though. He'd look fine in his wedding suit.

I tore at his shirt. The buttons popped through the holes and there was the wound, a burnt hole with ragged fleshy edges. It already smelled and I sucked in my breath. It needed a bandage.

I thought I could bind it with a piece of clean sheeting so I started ripping some. My hands were shaking. Well, I was shaking all over. I stopped right there and put my cheek against his face. My mouth touched on his. We were both cold.

I lifted him against me and wrapped the cloth around his back, then tied it over the wound. "Now it's all fixed," I said to him.

I reckon I thought he'd answer me, but there was just the rasping of J.C.'s saw outside.

🌺 MAC

I went out there with a coffin from Rowe's shop, an oak one already lined and hinged. J.C. stopped his work when I came up in the yard.

"I see you've started on it," I said to him. "Well, I was thinking you might want to use this one I've brought. I mean, Bethany might like it, seeing it came from out at the Malone's."

"That's right kind of you, Mac," J.C. said, "but I'm coming along here."

"Well," I said. "I was thinking you might want to make the little one instead. Rowe didn't have an infant size out there."

"What?" J.C. let the saw clang down on the frame he was making.

I should have known I'd be the one to tell him. "It's Caroline," I said.

"What about her?" He had his head bent like he'd rather take the blade than hear.

"Lord, J.C., your boy went to see Bethany this afternoon. He wanted to hold the baby for a minute and she let him. She shouldn't have but she did." He didn't stop me so I went ahead. "They were on the walk there at the house and he — well, Bethany says he just opened his arms and let her go. It wasn't that he threw her or anything. Bethany'd want you to know that."

"Oh Jesus," J. C. said.

"Anyhow, I was thinking you might want to use this coffin. The family's offering it to you."

"I'm obliged." He was looking at the house. Emma was standing in the back door. I reckon she could see more bad news on him.

"Let me help you get it in," I said.

We hoisted the box on our shoulders and carried it across the yard. Emma held the door open. Joel was there on the kitchen table, his face and chest covered with cloths that smelled of camphor, his pants and shoes still on. We put the coffin in the parlor and went back to the kitchen.

"Emma, the baby's gone, too," he said. "It's both of them."

She put her face in her apron but didn't make a sound.

"Ed'll help me get the saw horses to set it on," J.C. said to me. "I thank you for coming, Mac."

"Bethany wants this done tomorrow," I told them both.

"She's his wife. It's up to her, I reckon," J. C. said.

"She wants the burial out at Shiloh. We've got places out there."

Emma looked bad. Maybe she hadn't thought about having to bury him. See dirt dropping off a shovel.

"It's as good a place as any," J.C. said.

"Wilton Holmes will be doing the service. If you want anything special said, you'll have to let him know. The family's gathering at our house tonight, if you want to come sit with us."

They looked empty, like they didn't know what I was talking about, like they couldn't take it in.

"I don't know exactly what all's planned. The service is going to be at eleven tomorrow morning at Shiloh Cemetery — well, I've said that. I was thinking maybe you'd want to bring Joel down to our house later on since that's where Bethany is. I don't know what the proper thing is but it doesn't seem right to me for him to be out here and his little baby with us. The truth is Bethany won't let anybody touch the baby, not yet anyway. She's still holding it so I can't see as she's going to be willing to bring it out here."

"Charlotte always hated him," Emma said.

"And he wasn't fond of her," J.C. said.

They looked at each other, then J.C. went on: "But that's where Bethany is and he loved her and that baby better than anything."

"Well, you folks decide," I said. "If you want to come, with or without him, you'll be welcomed."

I let myself out the kitchen door. Passing J.C.'s workplace, I remembered we never decided about the coffin for the baby but I didn't go back and ask.

CHAPTER TWENTY-ONE

🌺 PREACHER WILTON

Food started coming right at suppertime. Women up and down the street simply picked up part of their supper off the table and took it to Charlotte's kitchen door after Hazel Watson reported the terrible news to the bank tellers who were on their way out at quitting time. They told everybody they saw and since they went in opposite directions, word fanned out and spread quickly. By dark, everybody in Whitney knew the baby was dead and most of them had gotten the full story and were shaking their heads and holding their own children too tight.

When Milly and I got to the house, all the Malones were there except Charlotte's sister Rose and hers who live a distance away and were coming first thing in the morning. I sat in the parlor on the sofa next to Bess who kept patting my hand like I was the one grieving. Maybe she had some idea how hard being the preacher is at times like that. I was waiting to be let into Bethany's room because she wasn't coming down. According to Bess, she hadn't given up the baby either.

I didn't know what I was going to say when I got up there. I was thinking maybe I should ask if she wanted to pray. That

comforts some, mostly old people though, who like long conversa-
tional prayers that explain things to God but don't expect Him to
fix it all. Bethany wasn't like that. Besides, none of this could be
fixed. It just had to be lived through. That's what I'd tell her.

"Wilton, honey, Charlotte's wanting you," Bess said, patting on me again.

Charlotte was standing in the door, her face all streaked
and swollen like she'd just had a good cry. Her mouth looked like
a bright red scar and her eyes seemed more deep and staring than
usual.

"Tell her I'm down here, too," Milly said to Charlotte. I
was glad she was talking to Charlotte instead of to me. I didn't
want to hurt her feelings but I thought this should be between
Bethany and her pastor.

I went upstairs and knocked on the only closed door on
the hall. She didn't answer, so I opened it and peeped in. Bethany
was sitting in a rocking chair near the window with the baby in
her arms. The baby's skin looked dark and waxy like a poorly
made doll might.

I cleared my throat and said: "This is the hardest time
you'll ever have in your life."

"I certainly hope so." She was barely rocking like she
intended to get up any minute and put a sleeping baby to bed.

"I want to talk to you about the service." I sat down on the
bed with my Bible on my knees. "We can go several ways.
Separate funerals or one. In the church or at the graveside."

"One funeral," Bethany said. "At the graveside." She
sighed then and looked out at the night. Stars were bunching up
above the house across the street. "Joel didn't go to church but
once in all the time I knew him and that was to marry me. He
needn't go again."

"At the cemetery then." I opened the Bible on my lap. I
can tell you just having it there was a comfort to me. "I'll read
from Holy Scripture, something of your choosing if you'd like.
Then I'll say a few words, nothing that will keep folks standing
long. Then a prayer. Maybe the Lord's Prayer at the end?"

"You could read that part about Jesus and the little children," she said. I heard a sob catch in her throat. She was holding the baby's head in her hand.

"That's good. There's a passage in Jeremiah I think would be fitting, too. Was there something Joel particularly liked that you know of?"

She shook her head.

"The Twenty-third Psalm is always good," I told her.

"I keep losing people," she said all of a sudden. "Why is that?"

"I don't know."

She wasn't looking at me but I felt she expected an answer.

"I do know some people have heavy crosses," I said. "I don't believe God gives us more than we can bear, though."

"Joel had more than he could bear," she said.

"Well, I suppose that's true. I was saying that about you."

She looked at me then. Her face was as dry and empty as a mask.

"Milly's here. She'd like to come up and speak," I said.

"All right." She started rocking again.

I got up and started toward her but as I neared I could feel her getting ready to spring. I backed off. "I'll tell Milly," I said. "And Bethany, if you need me anytime, day or night, you send somebody to get me."

She was still rocking when I left.

🌸 CHARLOTTE

I was with Bethany when Milly and Mama came up with the news that the Calders had arrived with Joel's body.

"Charlotte, you'll have to come down and speak. You can't let them come and go without a word," Mama said. How she'd managed to get up the stairs on her swollen legs I'll never know.

"They've brought saw horses and they're moving furniture to set it up in front of the fireplace," Milly said.

"Who in God's name told them they could bring him here?" I wanted to know.

"I did," Bethany said. "I told Mac to tell them."

"Well, he must have lost his mind, doing what a person in your state tells him."

"Well, now they're here, somebody's got to go down there and talk to them," Mama said. "You know they're grieving, too."

"Then you and Milly will have to do it," I said. "Tell them I'm indisposed." I looked at Bethany and the baby. "Tell them we both are."

After they'd gone, I shut the door and said to her, "I know we have to do this however you want it, but I don't have to approve."

"It would help if you'd try," she said.

"I can't." I leaned against the door, about as tired as I've ever been. "There're other things we've got to do, honey. We've got to lay out the baby. It's almost too late as it is."

"I know," Bethany said. "She's not soft anymore." Tears glinted in the corners of her eyes and her mouth curled downward, holding back a cry.

"Let me run a basin of warm water and we'll give her a nice bath," I said. "It's got to be done."

"Will you help me?"

"Of course I will," I told her.

Together we bathed the baby, powdered and diapered her. There was a narrow red line of rash on the roll of fat where her diaper had rubbed her leg and I almost reached for the cream Fred had prescribed before I remembered it didn't matter anymore.

The wound had made part of her face purple, like a large irregular birthmark, but she was still beautiful. Bethany combed the fuzz of auburn hair and curled it around her damp finger. Then we dressed her in a little batiste dress, blue with delicate cutwork and tiny pink and white rosettes about the neck. We didn't put her booties on.

"Let's take her downstairs," I said when we were finished. Then I remembered we hadn't done anything about a coffin. Well, we could move the crib down there and get a coffin in Lawrence in the morning. I'd just go down and get Mac to bring the crib.

But then I saw Bethany intended to go with me so I let her go in front. She was carrying Caroline. Downstairs, we passed startled neighbors in the hall, then went through the arched entrance to the parlor where the family was gathered. Mac and J.C. were standing in front of the coffin but they stepped aside when they saw her coming. They pulled back slowly, it seemed to me, like they were opening the gates of hell. She stopped between them and they both put out hands to catch her if she fell. She didn't, although her face blanched and a wildness came in her eyes. I knew that face. I'd seen it during her labor, a twisted look of pain so deep and wrenching it was hardly human.

"Oh," she said. "Oh, Joel."

Then she leaned over, her lips brushing his face a moment before she straightened and, with a sigh, lay their daughter in his arms.

🏵 MAC

The next morning J.C. and Ed Calder came to take the coffin out to Shiloh. I helped them ease the box onto the back of the truck. Ed stayed up there to hold it steady on the ride so it was J.C. and Emma in the cab. Bethany, Charlotte and the children got in the car with me. It was like going out to Shiloh of a Sunday morning except that nobody said a word.

Cars were parked along the road out there and after we stopped among them, people got out and waited to walk behind us up to the cemetery. Wilton was already standing in front of the grave Rowe had seen to the day before. There were ropes lying across the top and the raw soil piled at one end smelled fresh.

George and Trax and a few others came to help Ed so I waited with Charlotte and Bethany. The men slid the coffin off the truckbed onto their shoulders and carried it slowly ahead of us.

About half way there, Bethany said, "Wait!" and the procession stopped. The sky was clear blue and cloudless, almost like a fall morning, and the trees in the churchyard were still. We all held our breath. "I have to see them again," she said.

Charlotte nodded so the men set the coffin on the ground and George pried it open. The lid groaned before it gave.

She leaned down to them with her black skirt floating in the dirt. "Oh, my precious baby," she said and put her hand on the little head. "Oh, Joel." She leaned closer and whispered but I heard as clear as day. "You watch out for her, you hear?" she said. When it didn't seem like she was going to move, I went over and lifted her away. I held her shoulders while George and Ed fastened the lid again.

"Charlotte," she said then. "Come with me." And the two of them went on ahead.

Wilton read:
"Thus says the Lord:
     'A voice is heard in Ramah,
          lamentation and bitter weeping.
    Rachel is weeping for her children;
          she refuses to be comforted for her children,
          because they are not.'
"Thus says the Lord:
    'Keep your voice from weeping,
          and your eyes from tears;
    for your works shall be rewarded,
    says the Lord,
     and they shall come back from the land of the enemy.
    There is hope for your future,
    says the Lord,
          and your children shall come
          back to their own country."

❧ EMMA

You bring a child into the world. You wrest him free of your own body and set him out there all alone. Some kind of trust makes you do it, a belief you can't even speak of. You hold a baby to your heart and see him an infant always. You don't think he'll ever die.

❧ PREACHER WILTON

Rose's daughter Susan was singing. Her voice was clear and sweet and you could almost see it rising like a drift of smoke in the air. Emma Calder, who always seemed apart to me, leaned into her husband at the chorus and he wrapped his arm around her, holding her steady.

"Safe in the arms of Jesus," Susan sang. "Safe from corroding care, Safe from the world's temptations, Sin cannot harm me there!"

I can tell you it was sad and when the last note floated over us like a cry, I could hardly speak. I did though. I read the scripture from Mark about Jesus blessing the little children "for of such is the kingdom of God" and then I preached on it a few minutes. I told about the tribes of Israel, Rachel's lost children, and tied it in with the New Testament reading. I was going right along until Milly nudged me from behind and I saw everybody was getting hot and fidgety. I came to a quick conclusion that avoided mention of murder and suicide. Then I said the Twenty-Third Psalm like I'd planned.

What I couldn't do was pray. I got started like always, going deep like I did every Sunday morning, but then in my heart, I faltered. Words I'd normally say like faith and peace and comfort seemed puny and useless. I looked up at the bowed heads thinking that seeing them would make the words sound right but instead I saw what we were doing, the result of a terrible, terrible act and right there I had a doubt. It came over me like raging water and I couldn't get my breath. I tell you, I had to stop right there. I waited a little and cleared my throat, then asked them join in the Lord's Prayer.

Their voices filled the spaces around me. It was like being lifted up, buoyed above the flood. I could pick out Charlotte, a strong, serious voice like she was performing, and then Mac, full of resonance, doing his part. I could hear Milly behind me breathless, almost in a whisper. The combined voices of the others ebbed and flowed around me and I felt my doubt go with them. Then I heard a separate sound, Bethany's voice trembling out of the depths, drawing us to her. It was, I thought, the sound of Rachel weeping.

CHAPTER TWENTY-TWO

🌹 MENA

There come a steady stream to get their dishes. Folks all the time steppin up to the back door, not wantin to bother none. They ask how the family doin, soft like we still watchin over the dead. Bethany, she laid out on the glider like that other time, lookin like she the one passed, don't hardly move less somebody come to the front, then she sit up and act decent. I seen her tryin. That was after the milk.

Law, we had us a time! Miss Charlotte she too crazy to think and Bethany in grief so bad she don't hardly feel nothin. A day and a night done passed since she fed that baby when they come back from the buryin at Shiloh. By that time she all achy and swoll up. Done leaked all down her dress. I heats up rags in a pan of hot water and puts them on her and her just bawlin. It makes the milk come like I knowed it would but by mornin she swolled up agin. Miss Charlotte, she try to get her to work it out but she don't want to touch herself and I can't see as I blame her none. I keeps warmin them rags and she get some relief from it. Take days of tryin and her bawlin so hard she can't hardly see. She be right pitiful.

🌸 MAC

By the end of dog days, a hot blanket had spread over the South and nobody seemed to have the energy to stir under it. The tobacco market opened as usual and the price was better than we expected but in our family there wasn't much celebrating. Everybody was too worn out. Besides, none of us trusted our luck anymore even when the corn had made a decent crop and the early cotton was bringing a fair price. Things at the mill looked right good for a change and the bank was holding steady, too.

Of course, Charlotte's head was churning with plans. She's the kind that wants to get on with things, never mind the heat. Bethany couldn't lie there forever, she told me, and her job at the bank, well, that had been all right under the circumstances but now the circumstances were different. She wanted Bethany to go to college.

I saw her reasoning. After all, she was just eighteen years old, the right age for college especially considering how the Depression had slowed people down.

"Why, eighteen is young," Charlotte said. "Eighteen is a girl getting ready for a dance or trying on twenty pairs of shoes at Broydan's. It's dreaming of marrying somebody rich."

"Like you did, I reckon," I said to her.

"I want to know if we can still afford it, that's all." She was getting on her gown at the foot of the bed. "I don't want to be talking to your sister about her going up to Richmond to college and then find out we can't manage it."

"It's got to be her idea," I said. "I wouldn't be writing to people about it yet."

She got in bed beside me. "I'm talking about a little note to Lois, Mac. I'm not writing to the president of Harvard, for heaven's sake." She turned on her side away from me. "I don't see why, if you're not willing to actually help with this, you couldn't at least be a little bit encouraging."

"It's just that Bethany's got to live her own life."

"What life, pray tell? She doesn't have a life! That's the point. She's got to get up and do something."

"Honey, maybe she's doing all she can right now." I put my hand on her shoulder and eased her over toward me. "We've got the money for whatever she decides."

"Well, thank God for that."

I slipped my hand into the neck of her gown. "I wish you'd relax. You're wound like a spring all the time."

I let my hand drift on down.

"Hey," she said in the dark.

"Don't you worry about a thing," I told her.

🌺 BETHANY

I could hear them! I woke up feeling a pulse in the air, a rhythm I recognized loose in the house. I remember how Mama's room use to smell when I was little and I'd go nestle next to her after Daddy was up. The bed smelled like roses, a heavy, musky scent. I thought that must be how Charlotte's room was, too. I didn't want to know. I couldn't bear any more sadness but I couldn't stand their happiness either.

Their bed was moving. It was a solemn clunk like somebody rapping on a door but soft and untroubling to the rest of the sleeping house.

I had to get out of there, I knew that. I wondered how the little house in the country looked all closed up in the dark, the shades pulled down against the moonlight. I kept intending to go out there. I needed to get Mama's china and find a place to store the furniture in case J.C. wanted to move somebody in before spring. I didn't think I could ever use the furniture but maybe Davey or Patsy would want it someday. Maybe Lizzie. Or I could give it all to Mena. That would be better than having it dryrot in a barn somewhere.

"Damn you to hell, Joel," I said aloud in the dark, then

clamped my hand over my mouth in horror. "I didn't mean it, God," I whispered. "I didn't." I couldn't let myself hate him.

🌿 J.C.

I divided the crop income with Ed and stowed my part in a little metal box in the bottom of the wardrobe. I don't have much faith in banks, not even the Bank of Whitney that's never closed a day. Besides I didn't want to go to town any more than I had to. Seeing people made me tune up no matter how I tried to steady myself. I wasn't going around town acting weepy, that's for damn sure.

I'll have to say Emma got some better. It was like knowing where Joel was calmed her some. She didn't have to worry about him anymore, didn't have to see him at the table or in the field. I remember one time when the boys were younguns and she came out to the barn where we were putting in. There was Joel up in the top and him about eight years old. He was like a little squirrel back then, quick and sturdy, not a fear in him. Well, she about had a conniption fit. "Get him down from there!" she yells at me and I'm on the second tier, halfway down with my knees shaking.

"It's all right, Mama," he calls to her. "See what I can do!" And there he goes, balancing on one foot, no hands, like I told him a hundred times not to do. He's so excited though, wanting to impress. Then I see him going over. Not a thing in the world I can do. But by damn, he catches himself, gets one hand on the rafter and manages to straighten himself out. I remember how proud he was she'd seen.

A few weeks after the funeral, I went out to Shiloh one Sunday and sat there while their cardboard fans wagged around me and Wilton Holmes preached on Jesus' miracle of healing a blind man. It seemed to me Preacher Wilton's sermon begged the question. I wanted to know exactly how he did it. Was there something in the clay? I don't believe in miracles, but when I got back to the house, I felt like I'd been eased a little. I thought I might go out to Shiloh again and I have.

All We Know of Heaven

CHAPTER TWENTY-THREE

🌺 CHARLOTTE

She started taking the car. Didn't ask or say where she was going, just took the keys off the hall table and went, usually late in the afternoon. She'd be gone a hour, maybe two, but as the days shortened she'd come home sooner, before dusk.

Wherever she went, she didn't seem the worse for it, but I still wanted to know. Every afternoon the question itched on my tongue but I stayed quiet, testing myself as much as Bethany. How long could either of us last — one not asking, the other not telling?

She's the one who gave in. When she came in the kitchen one evening to help with supper, she left a trail of dirt behind her everywhere she stepped. "Oh, it's so muddy out at Shiloh," she said, stopping to take her shoes off.

So that's it, I thought while she went to get the broom. She's out there talking to him like somebody demented. I kept on poking at the chicken I was frying.

"You went to the cemetery?" I asked her.

"Yes. It's Mama I go to see, Charlotte. Not him."

"But there they are, right side by side," I said. The chicken sputtered and popped a tiny burn on my cheek. "I thought it was a mistake all along, putting him out there among our own. Always reminding us."

"But it's my baby, too." She sounded weary and she still looked bad, so drawn and skinny she reminded me of her six-year-old self.

The burn on my cheek was sending out little spikes of heat. "Don't think I'll ever forget that," I said.

"I've decided to go to college after Christmas," she said.

"That soon?" I wanted her to go but I thought I'd be the one to convince her.

"I have to do something," she said.

"Well, not this very minute you don't." I forked up the chicken.

"Let me do this, Charlotte," she said to me. "Let me do it my way."

"As if that's not the way it's always been," I told her.

JOEL

Whispery. Like a rustle in the trees. A creek murmur. That's what their voices are like. You don't try to hear them. They just come. I want to tell you there's no crying. Crying is of the world.

J.C.

Emma and me went by to see her. That colored woman they keep showed us into the parlor and told us to take a seat. All the furniture looked slick so we stood. She came back in a bit and offered us a cup of coffee. I said no. Didn't give her our coats either so she'd see we didn't come to stay.

In a minute or two, Bethany came down. I didn't try to hug her. I thought maybe leaving I could, when I had time to get to the truck before I tuned up. She was standing there in front of us looking awkward like a little girl who don't know she's already a beauty.

I didn't have anything planned to say. I reckon I should of, knowing Emma wouldn't speak a word in that house, but I didn't. Looking at that girl, all I wanted was to drop to my knees and beg her to forgive me. I wanted to say all I regretted in his life and hers.

"Here," Emma said and stuck out the picture she was holding.

Bethany came closer to take it. They stood there, the picture between them so it looked like it was floating in the air between giving and receiving. "What is it?" Bethany asked and caught hold.

"It's a picture of Joel," I said. "He was near about a year old, wasn't he, Emma? Well, he must of been because he was sitting up so good, pulling up against things, too, if I remember correctly. Just before walking."

I couldn't look down at the picture but she did. She brought it close and stared at it. I watched her face. Her chin trembled a little and her eyes got wet.

"He looks just like Caroline," she said. She couldn't stop looking.

🌿 MENA

Bethany got it stuck up there on her mirror — sweet little smilin chile in a dress. Got somethin in his little hand, a little play pretty, maybe a rattle. Can't hardly see what it is. I been studyin on that picture some and I reckon Caroline was takin after him all right. Maybe he seen that. Maybe in his mind he can see what look like hard times comin for her. But that ain't for me to ponder on. Don't nobody know and never will.

Gets me to thinkin bout all them babies that died — like them in the Bible when old Herod sent his soldiers out lookin for little Jesus. And in the Old Testament, too, in the time of baby Moses. And how bout places like Sodom? There was babies in them towns ain't harmed a soul.

In slave times babies passed, born and died on them ships, and got dropped off the side. Never put their little feet on solid ground, free or slave. Lord have mercy.

Well, me and Watteau got ourselves five chil'ren, all growed up fine but one. The second, Malone, he died of the measles when he was just a knee baby. He be buried at AME Zion where all my family lies. Sister's boy Simon, he's out there, too.

People gets born and dies. Some lives short like my baby and Simon and little Caroline. They don't hardly get started good. Some lives long and ain't worth squat. Bethany, she done lived one whole life and her nothin but a chile. Now she got to start again. Can't nobody do it for her. It's hers alone.

✿ MILLY

"At least she's thinking about going to college," Charlotte told me while we were walking home from the drugstore. "And the house has been emptied out. J.C. took care of that. Told her he needed it for a tenant again, like that wasn't all it ever was."

"Wilton said he took the truck, too."

"Well, it was his. I wish he'd take every single reminder of Joel Calder in the world and burn it to bits."

"That wouldn't change anything," I told her. "I declare, Charlotte, you don't have a lick of patience."

"I'm patient when things go my way. It's when they don't, I get riled."

I had to smile, seeing I was getting my old friend back. "Well, life goes on," I said.

"It certainly does, even without Huey Long!" Charlotte said and we broke out laughing right there on the street.

"People are going to think we've gone crazy," I said. I was trying to pull myself together. It won't do for the preacher's wife to be caught making a fool of herself.

Charlotte locked arms with me just like we were school-girls and we sashayed along. She was still laughing. "That felt as good as anything I've done in a long time," she said when she got her breath. "Well, almost anything."

"Charlotte, you're terrible!" I said and we laughed again. I think we were relieved to think it was so.

All We Know of Heaven

Chapter Twenty-four

 BETHANY

Dear Olivia,

Are you ever coming home again? Say you are! At Thanksgiving or Christmas! Please! I don't have anybody to talk to here, you know that. Charlotte doesn't want to hear, she wants to think I've put him out of my mind. She doesn't even mention Caroline, like not calling her name will make me forget. I want to remember my baby, Livy, I just don't want it to hurt so much.

Before he went back to Chapel Hill, Douglas came up here with a bouquet of yellow roses. Can you imagine such a thing? A book, too. Poetry by Edna St. Vincent Millay, the saddest poems you've ever read. What was he thinking of? Now I've had a letter from him, just a note really, saying he's thinking about me. I want Douglas to keep his mind in Chapel Hill, that's what I want from him, but I can tell you Charlotte is thrilled about the roses — and the letter, too. He should have sent them to her!

I'm going to college after Christmas — to Altamont up in the mountains. It's near where Joel and I went on our honeymoon. Lord, that seems like ages ago. I think I must have been another person then but when I think about it, it still hurts like somebody sticking a knife in me. I want my baby, Livy. I want my life —

Oh please come to see me! Love, Bethany.

🌿 CHARLOTTE

According to Mac, we've told enough. That's the way men are. They hold on to feelings and don't try to figure out what can't be understood. Women worry a mystery, though. We lie in bed at night asking why and how a thing came to be.

Many nights I've thought maybe I should have left her with Warren Newell. Of course, there's no denying he was a drunk. Oh, he'd go to work, put on a clean shirt and a sharp looking suit, shine up his shoes, slick his hair. Do fine for a few weeks, then one night he'd come home with a sack of bootleg whiskey and that would be the end of it. I was right to rescue her from that.

But then before she was grown, there was Joel coming at her like white heat. I can't say he didn't love her, but what is love? It's how two people see each other, isn't it? Love is their vision of what they want, it's their struck chords. It's not what everybody else sees and hears. Love, I believe, happens somewhere low in the body — in the stomach where, as I recall, that churning, wanting feeling starts. We say it happens in the heart, but that's not so. The heart beats on when we've lost our appetite, when our breath comes in sighs, when we are reaching down into our new-found terror of being without. I've felt that, so I know.

🌿 WARREN

I can tell you I was a mite surprised when Charlotte come pushing through the door before I could get it open good. Well, the smell out there in the hall was pretty bad. I used to keep it cleaned up, scour the piss and such, but I won't able to do nothing by then. I've been down with a stroke, you see. It took one side so I have to drag my leg more than raise it and one arm's about useless. My mouth don't work right either so it stays half raw and sore from my wiping on it.

She set down in the one chair up there and looked around. The place was a mess, just a little room with a narrow bed and a table with a hotplate on it. A little sink in the corner. All I needed what with the window to look out of and the words of the picture show coming through the wall for company.

"I hear you've been sick," she says right loud like she thought I'd gone deaf, too.

I had to work my mouth to get it going. "I been . . . ailing. . . awhile," I said, about like that.

"I hear you've had a serious stroke. I hear you can't even get down the stairs anymore. You're stuck up here with nobody to do for you." Hearing her say it, it sounded pretty bad. I tried to keep my head from bobbing like it wants to do. "Well, I've been trying to think of some way to help you," she said.

With that, I just about busted out crying. I got to strangling on it, though, and she had to look around for something to give me. She ended up handing me her own handkerchief.

"I've been out to the County Home this morning and they've got a place. You'll be sharing a room, of course, but it's bigger than this and clean. You'll get your meals, clean clothes and any medicine you need."

She was trying to convince me when it sounded like paradise to me. I tried to tell her but no words come quick enough.

"I could carry you right now except I don't have anybody to help get you downstairs. I tell you what, Mac and I can come back and take you out there later this afternoon, before suppertime." She got up. "You're going to be fine, Warren."

"H-h-ha-ha-te me." I tried to remind her how it used to be.

"I used to," she told me. "But we're all too old for that now," she said.

❧ BETHANY

Lizzie was stuck playing Mary.

"Now that I'm out of high school and working at a job, I thought I wouldn't have to do this anymore," she said. We were getting her ready in the Sunday School classroom out at Shiloh.

I could remember when it was the biggest thing in the world.

"All of us wanted to be Mary," I reminded her.

"Well, that was when we were thirteen." Mama Bess's old shawl was refusing to drape over her head and shoulders right. "I've been Mary three times already. I told Mama this is the last Christmas, the very last."

"Then I guess it'll be Patsy's part," I said. Patsy had been the speaking angel for years. "I suppose Harry is still Joseph, too."

"Well, of course he is since Trax got married," Lizzie said. "Why, if it weren't for Malones there wouldn't be a pageant at all. I told Preacher Wilton he's got to get busy converting some new Baptists."

"You told him that?"

"I most certainly did. I said, 'Preacher, you've just got to get the missionary spirit around here because this is the last year for me'."

Just then we heard Milly playing "O Come All Ye Faithful" in the sanctuary, as solemn as a dirge.

"I could be Mary," I said. It surprised me I'd said it but then I didn't want to take it back.

"You wouldn't!" Lizzie said. "Would you really?"

"Of course, I will."

"But you — you've been married. What will people say?" Lizzie was getting out of the costume we'd been using for years.

"I don't care." I put Mama Bess's shawl around me. It was soft and smelled of her lavender sachets.

Lizzie got me into the long blue dress and pinned the shawl to my hair. "Oh," she said when she could step back to look. Then we hurried out through the cold night to join the procession lined up in the vestibule.

"Here, take this," she said and dropped a doll in my arms, then slipped away to find a seat.

How could I have forgotten there'd be a baby to hold?

🌸 CHARLOTTE

Milly was playing "O Little Town of Bethlehem." I saw Patsy go past leading the littler angels. I knew Davey would come later wearing the outfit I made out of my old silk bathrobe and a towel turban decorated with bits and pieces of costume jewelry. So I wasn't even looking until Mac nudged me and there going past was Bethany wearing the Mary costume with Mama's shawl framing her face. Her mouth was quivering and she was looking down but she walked steadily, carrying that bundled up doll baby in her arms.

I watched her kneel down there surrounded by little shepherds and angels, her cousin Harry standing behind looking like a reluctant Joseph. Patsy was bright in her wings, her blond hair a halo of light around her face.

I suppose they said all the words like Milly had rehearsed them. I suppose Davey was stifling an embarrassed grin when he marched in carrying his cigar box of myrrh. But I didn't truly see him. I could only look at her, my heart child, my Mary at the empty manger.

BETHANY

The doll was stiff in my arms but I made myself snuggle its little body close. Its porcelain head was cradled at my elbow. I could hear Wilton reading. I knew when he got to the part about swaddling clothes and the manger I was supposed to lay the baby down. I'd played this part before but now I knew it wasn't all neat and clean, Mary and Joseph off on a holiday. It was hot crushing pain and blood and cries. Then sleep. Finally sleep.

I put the doll in the straw and then the angels spoke and the shepherds came and the wise men brought gifts and everybody stood to sing. Their voices rose around me, flooding my head. I could have separated the sounds — I knew every voice — but I didn't want to. Instead I wanted to hear them like a single voice. It was "Joy to the World" they sang.

MAC

After everybody was in the house at Rowe's Crossing, the children out of their coats and the presents under the tree, I noticed Bethany was missing. She was out on the front porch.

"Aren't you cold?" I asked her. The lights from the Christmas tree were sparkling around us but the night beyond the porch was deep.

"Not yet. I was burning up in church."

"I was proud of you tonight," I told her. "So was Charlotte." I lit a cigarette.

A burst of laughter came from the parlor and we turned to watch through the window while Rowe did a jig his daddy had taught him years ago. It was amazing how agile he was. Behind him in the dining room, the women were bringing the soup tureen to the table. We were having oyster stew like always.

"You think my going to school is the right thing, don't

you?" she asked me.

"Yes, I do."

"I've never been away from home before, not like to college."

I was thinking about the house Charlotte took her from and the little tenant house not far from here. I reckon she was, too.

"But I feel like I've lived a whole lifetime already," she said.

"Well, you have."

"There's a torn place in me, Mac. I think it'll always be there. No matter who I love or how many children I have, there'll be the two of them holding onto my heart."

"I could tell you time heals everything," I said, "but I don't know that it does."

Lucille rapped on the window. "Yoo-hoo-o-o-o!" She motioned for us to come inside.

"Soup's on." My cigarette butt made a tiny orange spiral in the dark before it landed in the yard. "After awhile, we'll light the sparklers."

"Like old times," she said and gave me a hug.

"It's all right if you fall in love again," I told her. "You remember that. The best part of living is having somebody to care about."

BETHANY

Uncle George had a fancy new camera so after we finished supper and opened our presents, everybody gathered in the parlor to have their pictures taken. Uncle George took one of all of us in front of the tree. Then Mac took one so Uncle George could be in it. Then Mama Bess reminded them to take one for Trax who was spending Christmas with his wife's people. We could tell Aunt Lucille hated his being over in Lenoir County but she didn't say anything.

Charlotte wanted Uncle George to take one more picture. "One of us," she said. "Heaven only knows when the Woodard branch of this family will be together again."

She pulled Patsy in front of her and motioned for Mac and Davey to come close. "Now Bethany," she said. "Right here in the middle."

"I think it should be just you four," I said. They looked so beautiful standing there in front of Mama Bess's tree with the colored lights sparkling around them. My eyes filled up, seeing how perfect they were.

"Why no, we can't have a picture without you," Charlotte said in that way of hers. "Now come right here next to me."

And so I went.

+ RW

F
BRI

Bridgers, Sue Ellen.

All we know of
heaven.

$22.00

DATE			

12/96